LEFT BANK

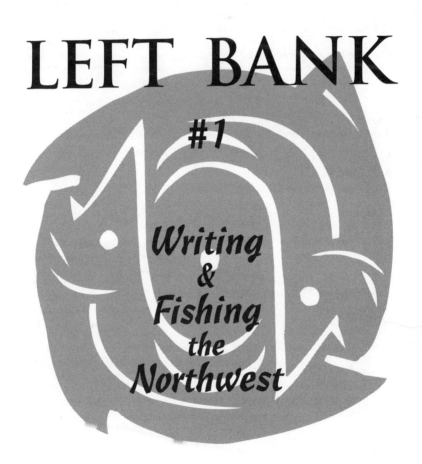

#1

*Writing
&
Fishing
the
Northwest*

BLUE HERON PUBLISHING, INC.
HILLSBORO, OREGON

Editor: Linny Stovall
Associate Editor: Stephen J. Beard
Publisher: Dennis Stovall
Staff: Mary Jo Schimelfenig, John Johnson, William Woodall
Advertising: Linny Stovall
Design: Dennis Stovall
Cover: Marcia Barrentine
Advisors: Ann Chandonnet, Madeline DeFrees, Katherine Dunn, Jim Hepworth, Ursula Le Guin, Lynda Sexson, J.T. Stewart, Alan Twigg, Shawn Wong

Editorial correspondence: Linny Stovall, Left Bank, Blue Heron Publishing, Inc., 24450 N.W. Hansen Road, Hillsboro, OR 97124. Submissions are welcome if accompanied by a stamped, self-addressed envelope. Otherwise they will not be returned. Subjects or authors must have a strong connection to the Pacific Northwest. Editorial guidelines are available on request (include SASE).

Left Bank, a magazine in book form, is published semiannually by Blue Heron Publishing, Inc., 24450 N.W. Hansen Road, Hillsboro, OR 97124. Subscriptions are $14 per year (postage included). Single issues are $7.95 (plus $1.50 s&h). Left Bank is distributed to the book trade and libraries in the United States by Consortium Book Sales and Distribution, 287 East Sixth Street, Suite 365, Saint Paul, MN 55101. In Canada, Left Bank is available through Milestone Publications Ltd., PO Box 35548, Stn. E, Vancouver, B.C. V6M 4G8.

Rights & permissions: "Cordova" excerpted with permission from *Out of the Channel: The Exxon Valdez Oil Spill in Prince William Sound*, Edward Burlingame Books, an imprint of HarperCollins, 1991. § "Be All You Can — Take Orders and Don't Think," Paul Richards. Reprinted with permission. First printed in *Mother Jones*. § "Duwamish" reprinted with permission. First published in *The Rest Is Silence*, R.P. Jones, Broken Moon Press, Seattle, WA, 1984. § "Haunted Waters" excerpted with permission from *Norman Maclean*, edited by James R. Hepworth, Confluence Press, 1988. § "An Interview With William Kittredge" reprinted with permission from *…When We Talk About Raymond Carver*, edited by Sam Halpert; Gibbs Smith, Publisher; 1991. § "Justice In Our Time" excerpted with permission from *Justice In Our Time: The Japanese Canadian Redress Settlement* by Roy Miki and Cassandra Kobayashi, Talonbooks and The National Association of Japanese Canadians, 1991. § "Last Stand" reprinted with permission from *Last Stand: Logging, Journalism, and the Case for Humility*, by Richard Manning; Gibbs Smith, Publisher, 1991. § "Magadan Luck" copyright © 1991 Nancy Lord. First published in *Uncommon Waters: Women Write About Fishing*, edited by Holly Morris, Seal Press, 1991. Reprinted with permission. § "If Poets Were Made;" "Sorry, We Don't Take Westerns;" "On Science Fiction" appeared first in *Writer's Northwest Handbook, 4th Edition*, 1991. Reprinted with permission.

Cover and inside art: Dennis Cunningham

LEFT BANK #1, Winter 1991
Copyright © 1991 by Blue Heron Publishing, Inc.

ISBN 0-036085-19-3
ISSN 1056-7429

CONTENTS

3

INTRODUCTION

THIS, THE NORTHWEST corner of North America, is not the Left Bank of '20s Paris, but like that legendary time and place, is a meeting ground for ideas of growing intensity and reach. Writers, artists, and idea vendors from this region have pushed their works into the consciousness of the East like a weather front sweeping off the Pacific and over the Great Divide. The effect on the intellectual climate has been profound.

LEFT BANK is a magazine that seeks to penetrate the issues of our time — the questions about the use and misuse of our lands, our world's natural resources, disappearing species, the management and repair of changes wrought in our lives by technology. It will showcase the thinkers now debunking the notion that our corner of the continent is the "last best place," telling the new stories of the Left Bank region with truth and artistry. We agree with Sallie Tisdale, author of the recently released book *Stepping Westward,* who says, "I began to see the Northwest for what it was. I realized the myth I'd been fed all my life, about the pioneers — how they were good and heroic people, how progress was important and that trees [would] be around forever — was largely nonsense."

In LEFT BANK #1: *Writing and Fishing the Northwest,* we present writers you have read and writers you've never heard of. They touch on subjects likely to rear their heads somewhere down stream in our lives. Here they offer insights into fishing as metaphor and writing as the naming of truth.

In "Last Stand," Richard Manning shows us the perils of writing as he investigates big timber companies and loses his newspaper job while the paper wins awards for his reporting. "Justice In Our Time" exposes racism — Japanese Canadians, many of whom were fisherman, fight for recognition of crimes committed against them by their government in WWII, finally winning reparations. In "Duwamish," R.P. Jones pays poetic homage to Richard Hugo who died on the day they'd planned to fish.

Other pieces celebrate the joys of new directions, the contradictions of regionalism, and the rewards and tyranny of poesy and prose.

We invite you to enjoy.

— The Editors

FOREWORD

BY CRAIG LESLEY

IMAGINE EARLY APRIL at Celilo Village on the Columbia River. The people have gathered in the long house to celebrate the salmon's return. As the feast begins, the Chief raises his glass of clear river water. "Choos!" he pronounces, and all the people raise their glasses to drink the water young men have ladled from metal buckets moments earlier. This spring, as for thousands of springs, they celebrate the river.

MY GRANDMOTHER'S KITCHEN window overlooked the Columbia, and I always considered it my river. Of all its wonders, nothing struck me with such awe as Celilo Falls did, and I spent many afternoons and evenings gazing at its power. As the fishermen dipnetted from their perilous scaffolds or rode the tiny cable car across the whitewater to Rhythm Rock, I marveled.

Everyone lost when the floodgates closed on The Dalles Dam and its backwaters drowned Celilo Falls. This was a turning point for the traditional Native people along the river. Most were displaced, scattered in the name of progress. In *Winterkill* I wrote about some of these changes, and then intended to write a ranch novel set in Eastern Oregon. But every time I drove the Columbia, it pulled at my heart. Unfinished business.

I MET DAVID SOHAPPY at one of the Celilo Salmon Festivals and admired his wisdom, the way he lived in harmony with the river. Spiritual leader of the River People, David held to the old ways, and I was astonished and disturbed to consider that he had been sentenced to five years in federal prison for practicing his beliefs, following the laws of his "Maker."

At the festival that year, they served "lok-lok," fish head soup, and

David explained that by eating the salmon eye, one could see like the salmon. That struck me as a wonderful metaphor for the "seeing" involved in writing. The writer tries to see what the casual observer does not, then presents it with force and clarity so others can see it as well.

In *River Song*, I intended to portray the lives and values of those Native people who remained on the Columbia after the dams had destroyed their villages and fishing sites. I wanted the traveller through the Gorge to see more than the spectacular landscapes and bright sails of the windsurfers. I wanted to present the white styrofoam floats the Indian fishermen and women use to mark their nets, the huddled buildings and trailers on the "in lieu" fishing sites, the flimsy scaffolds still used for traditional dipnetting. Most of all, I hoped readers would understand that this river culture has continued for thousands of years, maintaining a harmony with the river that deserves recognition and respect.

"Some of the fish get funny looking," the fishermen remarked from time to time. "Some of the salmon, we won't eat." They'd shrug and return to their nets. "Bad stuff in the water."

In the Northwest, a stronghold of environmental awareness, these are startling words. I've seen the polluted rivers in other parts of the country and have even felt smug about the relative cleanliness of the water here. But the Native fishermen have expressed caution. When I think of the radioactive leakage at Hanford, the toxins released from plants and mills along the Columbia, the sewage spills in the Willamette, I wonder what was in that glass of water the Chief held.

"The solution to pollution is dilution" runs an old engineering adage, but we better not believe it. The solution is not to pollute — period. At Clackamas Community College where I work, the environmental science people have painted small fish designs near the storm drains along with the words "Dump no Waste. Drains to Stream." The message is clear: Don't put in oils, antifreeze, gasoline.

What we practice in private life — recycling and environmental consciousness — must carry over into our public lives as well. The writers must raise their voices against those forces that would dam, and pollute and destroy. What did the Northwest look like one hundred years ago? Think of it now. The Columbia and other rivers are miracles, but fragile ones, and must be protected.

The first issue of Left Bank celebrates the relationship of the writer to fishing and water. Working on *River Song*, I had the privilege of being with people who treated the water as a living being. Imagine the inside of that longhouse again where one of the tribal leaders is speaking: "This land that we're standing on is the body of our Mother. The rivers running through are her blood. She deserves our care and respect."

Amen.

HAUNTED BY
WATERS

BY WALLACE STEGNER

THE WRITING CAREER of Norman Maclean is a phenomenon. A retired English professor from the University of Chicago at the age of seventy begins, secretly and almost shamefacedly, to write down the stories of his youth that he has told his children. He produces three stories of such unfashionable length and kind — among other defects, "they have trees in them" — that no magazine or trade publisher is interested. Through the influence of friends, they are finally brought out by the University of Chicago Press, which never published any fiction before that and so far as I know has published none since.

This slim book, virtually without reviews or advertising, finds its way into hands that pass it on to other hands. Fly fishermen discover it first, with delight, but others besides fishermen respond to it. A little group of admirers forms and spreads. A second printing is needed, then a third, then a paperback edition. By word of mouth a reputation is born. Now, ten years after his first and only fictions saw print, this author of three stories is an established name, an authentic western voice, respected and imitated, and books are being written about him.

Why? How? Every writer and publisher wishes he knew. The usual channels of publicity and criticism had virtually nothing to do with it. Neither did literary fashion, for that, along with the orthodoxies of contemporary short story form, is simply ignored in these stories.

For one thing, they are "realistic," and realism, as everyone knows, was long since left to the second-raters. For another, they are about the West, an environment of broad hats and low foreheads, a place traditionally short of thought and with only rudimentary feelings. For still another, they are about a *historical* West, Montana in the years during and just after World War I, a West that was less a society than a passing phase of the frontier; and they contain some of the mythic feeling and machinery, the crudeness, the colorful characters, and the ox-stunning fist fights made all too familiar by horse opera.

Don't look here for the economy and precision that have marked the short story at least since Joyce and in some ways since Poe. The characteristic modern short story starts as close to its end as it can. It limits itself to a unified action, often a single scene, and to the characters absolutely essential to that action. It covers the time and space required, no more, and picks up the past, insofar as it needs it, in passing. Ibsen perfected that "uncovering" technique in his plays a hundred years ago, rediscovering for both drama and fiction Aristotle's three unities.

But two of Maclean's stories spread across whole summers, and the third contains an entire life. In all three the action moves around—mountains to town, town to the Big Blackfoot to Wolf Creek, camp to cafe, cafe to bar. Instead of a rigidly limited cast of characters, whole communities inhabit these tales: rangers, cooks, dynamiters, packers, pimps, whores, waitresses with and without freckles, bartenders, barflies, family, in-laws, small-town doctors, horses, and coyote-killing dogs. Around their discursive actions a world grows up. Inclusion, not exclusion, is the intention; amplitude, not economy, is the means.

Furthermore, this writer talks to his readers, guesses at the motivations of characters, sums up, drops one-liners of concentrated observation and wisdom. He is garrulous and personal. The puppeteer shows his hands and feet. No wonder he couldn't find an orthodox publisher.

It is instructive to note what is not here, but more so to note what is. All three of these stories, even "Logging and Pimping," the first-written, shortest, and least-satisfying, grow on re-reading. The two longer ones grow a great deal. Things that looked only reported turn out to have been *rendered.* Throwaway lines reveal unexpected pertinence, discursiveness that we first forgave as naivete has to be reappraised as deep cunning. Maybe Maclean knew fully what he was doing, maybe he only moved by instinct sharpened through years of studying literature, maybe his hand was guided by love and nostalgia for places and people long left behind. However he did it, he made a world.

The Montana of his youth was a world with the dew on it. Perhaps the time of youth always has dew on it, and perhaps that is why we respond to Maclean's evocation of his. But I lived in Montana, or close to it, during those same years, and it was a world younger, fresher, and more touched with wonder and possibility than any I have since known. After seventy years, I still dream it; and when it is revived by these stories it glows with a magical light, like one of those Ansel Adams photographs that are more magnificent than the scenes they pretend to represent.

The remembered and evoked world of barely-touched wilderness and barely-formed towns has, for all its primitiveness, violence, and freedom, an oddly traditional foundation. A raw society, it offers to growing boys mainly a set of physical skills — riding, shooting, fishing, packing, logging, fire-fighting, fist-fighting — and a code to go with them. The hero, the admired and imitated person, is one who does something superlatively well. To fail at a skill, if you try your best, is unfortunate but respectable; to fail in nerve or trying is to merit contempt.

It is absolutely right that the seventeen-year-old Norman Maclean of "USFS 1919" should model himself on Bill Bell, the best ranger, best packer, best all-around mountain man, and best fighter in the Bitterroot country. It is right that in "Logging and Pimping" a grown-up Norman Maclean should half kill himself keeping up with the sadistic logger-pimp Jim. It is right that in "A River Runs Through It" he and his brother, trained by their father in fly fishing and its mysteries, should reserve their deepest contempt for bait fishermen. Skill is both competitive and proud. As the basis of a code, it can be harshly coercive on attitudes and conduct.

Also, it is not enough. Unaccompanied by other more humane qualities, skill can produce a bully like Jim or a tinhorn like the cook. The code goes beyond skill to character; for those who subscribe to it, it defines a man. A man for young Norman Maclean is neither mouthy nor finicky; he is stoical in the face of pain; he does not start fights but he tries to finish them; he does what his job and his morality tell him to do. But he cannot get by on mere skill. He needs something else, some decency or compassion that can only be learned from such sources as the boys' preacher father. In the beginning, he reminds his son, was the Word.

I knew a few P.K.'s in my youth. Most were Scottish. All had to learn to reconcile that harsh, limited, demanding code of their frontier society with the larger codes in which grace and personal salvation ultimately lie. Norman Maclean learned that. His brother Paul, with more skills, with every advantage except the capacity to transcend the code of his place and time, did not.

I speak as if the stories were about real people. I think they are. Maclean gives us no reason to make a distinction between real and fictional people. The stories are so frankly autobiographical that one suspects he hasn't even bothered to alter names. The only thing that has happened to young Maclean's experience is that it has been recollected in tranquillity, seen in perspective, understood, and fully felt. The stories are a distillation, almost an exorcism.

The Maclean boys grew up in a world "overbearing with challenges" and dominated by the code. Sent to the fire-watch station on Grave Peak, sure that he has been sent off as punishment for his dislike of the cook, young Maclean responds by trying to do the job so well, in spite of rattlers, grizzlies, and lightning storms, that Bell will have to admit he has been unjust. (Bell doesn't; he takes the performance for granted.) Pulling all day on the end of a seven-foot crosscut whose other end is in the hands of a bully determined to put him down, Maclean would die on the saw rather than admit he was even tired. Told to go for the money if a fight breaks out, he goes for it, though he knows he will get his face busted. Commanded to take his impossible brother-in-law fishing, he and Paul do, though they would rather drown him.

In every case the reward for faithfulness is acceptance. The logger-pimp Jim learns enough respect for Maclean to make him a "pal." Bill Bell, making up for the whole unsatisfactory summer, asks him to join the crew again next year. And the women caretakers of the impossible brother-in-law let him know without saying it (they are no more mouthy than their men) that he has done his duty, that the failure is not his.

These rites of passage through observance of the code, these steps toward a simplistically-understood manhood, dominate both "Logging and Pimping" and "USFS 1919," and are present in "A River

Runs Through It." But they are not enough to account for the astonishing success of Maclean's little book. The fact is, the title story contains everything that the other two do, and far surpasses them, transcends them. It flies where they walk. Where they are authentic, humorous, ironic, observant, and much else, "A River Runs Through It" is both poetic and profound.

In the other stories the skills under discussion are work skills from a half-forgotten time. They are recreated as lovingly as Melville recreates the boats, the gear, the try-works, and the rest of his cetology. They pack the crevices of the narrative with a dense exposition of *process*. Getting up from reading, we could make a pass at fighting a forest fire or balancing the load on a mule.

But fishing with a dry fly, which is the skill that gives both meaning and form to "A River Runs Through It," is not labor but an art, not an occupation but a passion, not a mere skill but a mystery, a symbolic reflection of life.

Fly fishing renounces the pragmatic worms and hardware of the meat fishermen. It is truly an art, "an art that is performed on a four-count rhythm between ten and two o'clock." It calls for coordination, control, and restraint more than for strength. To do it right you need not only skill but the imagination to think like a fish. It has its rituals and taboos, and thus is an index to character like the code, but far subtler. There is no clear distinction between it and religion. It takes place in wild natural places, which for Maclean mean awe, holiness, respect; and in water, which he feels as the flow of time.

Like the lesser skills, fly fishing has its arrogance. Witness Paul's response to Izaak Walton's *Compleat Angler*. Not only is Walton a bait fisherman but the sonofabitch can't even spell "complete." The pride of a supreme artist, plus an unswerving adherence to the code, is a recipe for disaster, a fatal flaw. Despite his artistry and his grace, Paul is one who cannot be helped because he will not accept help. Some saving intelligence, a capacity to see beyond or around the code, saves Paul's brother, but his brother cannot save Paul.

So is this a story of *hubris* in the Bitterroots, of a young god destroyed by pride? If it is, why all that other stuff the story contains — all that tawdry story of looking after the incompetent, mouthy brother-in-law, all that bawdy farce of the whore Old Rawhide and the sunburned backsides? If this is a story of pathetic or tragic failure, why is it cluttered up with so much exposition of the art of fishing, so many stories of fishing expeditions, so many homilies from the preacher father, so many hints about the relations of Norman Maclean with his wife's family? An impressive story as it stands, would this be even more impressive if it were cleaned up, straightened up, and tucked in?

I will tell you what I think. I only think it, I don't know it; but once when I suggested it in Norman Maclean's presence he didn't deny it. Perhaps, like Robert Frost, he thinks a writer is entitled to anything a reader can find in him. Perhaps I persuaded him of something he hadn't realized. More likely, he knew it all along.

The fact is, or I think it is, that this apparently rambling yarn is made with the same skill that Paul displays while fishing the Big Blackfoot, the same deliberation and careful refusal to hurry, the same reading of the water. "It is not fly fishing if you are not looking for the answers to questions," the author says, and this is big water demanding every skill.

Listen to how Paul fishes — (this is early in the story, and may be taken as a forecast of what is to come):

> *The river above and below his rock was all big Rainbow water, and he would cast hard and low upstream, skimming the water with his fly but never letting it touch. Then he would pivot, reverse his line in a great oval above his head, and drive his line low and hard downstream, again skimming the water with his fly. He would complete this grand circle four or five times, creating an immensity of motion which culminated in nothing if you did not know, even if you could not see, that now somewhere out there a small fly was washing itself on a wave. Shockingly, immensity would return as the Big Blackfoot and the air above it became iridescent with the arched sides of a great Rainbow.*
>
> *He called this "shadow casting," and frankly I don't know whether to believe the theory behind it — that the fish are alerted by the shadows of flies passing over the water by the first casts, so hit the fly the moment it touches the water. It is more or less the "working up an appetite" theory, almost too fancy to be true, but then every fine fishermen has a few fancy stunts that work for him and for almost no one else. Shadow casting never worked for me....*

But if shadow casting never worked for the fisherman Norman Maclean, it works marvelously well for the fictionist. He fills the air with flies that never really settle, he dazzles us with loops of glittering line, he keeps us watching Old Rawhide, who does not matter at all, and the brother-in-law, who matters only in that he demonstrates the lack of everything that makes Paul special, and he keeps us from watching Paul, who does matter. Then, on page 102 of a 104-page story, the fly settles, and we strike at what we have been alerted to but have not been allowed to anticipate.

Bluntly, brutal, in a few hundred words, the important part of the story is ended with Paul's life; the shadow falls suddenly on a tale that has been often sunny, even facile. Time comes down like a curtain, what has been vibrantly alive is only remembered, we are left hollow with loss, and we end in meditation on the Big Blackfoot in the cool of the evening, in the Arctic half-light of the canyon, haunted by waters.

The ending is brought off with such economy only because it was earlier obscured by all the shadow casting. A real artist has been fishing our stream, and the art of fishing has been not only his message but his form and his solace. An organ should be playing Bach's *Es Ist Vollbracht.*

"A River Runs Through It" is a story rooted in actuality, in known people and remembered events. But is a long way from a limited realism. It is full of love and wonder and loss, it has the same alternations of sunshine and shadow that a mountain stream has, and its meaning can be heard a long way from its banks. It is an invitation to memory and the pondering of our lives. "To me," Maclean remarks in his introduction, "the constant wonder has been how strange reality has been."

Fisherman or not, who is not haunted by waters?

CORDOVA

BY JOHN KEEBLE

WE WERE IN CORDOVA, a town as different as it can be from Valdez. It had a population of about 2,600 that swelled annually to about 5,000 during the peak of fishing season, when cannery workers and Prince William Sound fishing permit holders who live elsewhere during the winter arrived. Valdez had a steadier population of about 3,500, and a city budget at least six times the size of Cordova's, thanks in no small part to the property tax levied against the Alyeska terminal. In Valdez, occupations are apportioned among education, small business, fishing, tourism, the Coast Guard, and Alyeska. A good percentage of the people put in their hours and go home to their climate-controlled houses. Valdez is a microcosm of the sharp occupational tensions one finds in most American cities. Tourism and fishing have long been at odds with oil shipping. With the oil spill, the differences became conflicts.

In Cordova, everything is directly or indirectly addressed to fishing. Before the oil spill, divisions in the community tended to take the form of close-in body punching followed by clinches, as if among relatives. Although Cordova itself, protected by the sound's prevailing westward currents and Knowles Head to the northeast and Hawkins Island just across the bay, had not been struck by the slick (nor had the nearby, prolific fishing grounds off the Copper River Delta), the town depended upon all of the sound for its sustenance. In response to the spill, the townspeople formed a solid wall of protest. On the Tuesday after, the first of several town meetings found the high-school gym packed with upwards of 2,000 hissing, hooting, contentious people, furious over the lack of action. The Exxon and Alyeska representatives arrived late and wanted to leave early. They couldn't.

Through loss, Cordovans' feeling for the beauty of their place and for the way their lives were entwined with the sound had taken on new force. Fishermen have a not always deserved reputation for being roughnecks, or cowboys of the sea, who dump their trash and pump out sewage into the water, who catch all manner of things besides fish, and who sometimes cut loose their damaged nets and let them float to the bottom, where they became ghost nets. Made of plastic, they trap fish forever. Now, it was not uncommon to hear the crustiest of fishermen say, "We should have been paying attention," or "The environmentalists were right." They also resented the way Exxon, especially at the beginning, had treated them as incidental. The question, finally, would be to what extent Cordova and its fishermen could form new alliances or renew old ones with other fishing interests, environmentalists, tourism interests, and independent oil shippers, such as Chuck Hamel, and what steps they could take to counter the inherent imbalance in power between themselves and the oil companies.

At the moment, Richard Newman and I, each of us outsiders, were becoming aware of what Cordova already knew. We sat in the loft of the Killer Whale, a delicatessen-style restaurant that operated in the same building as the Orca Book and Sound. Valdez had no bookstore, and this one in Cordova, though small, had a stock that ran from bestsellers to esoteric literature, philosophy, and natural history. It bespoke the community. The store was also a center of oil spill response in the town, one of many private establishments where the margin between the conduct of business and community action grew so thin as to be invisible. The owner of the deli, Jeff Bailey, and the owners of the bookstore, Susan Ogle and Kelly Weaverling, husband and wife, were involved in the response. Ogle had been the first director of Cordova's Oil Spill Disaster Response Office (COSDRO). Since the fifth day of the spill Weaverling had coordinated an effort to rescue oiled wildlife — first birds, then birds and otters. While Richard Newman and I were talking, volunteers were busy pounding together plywood bins to make what Kelly hoped would be the Cordova Otter Rescue Center just across the street, a place to treat the animals Valdez could no longer handle. Paths had been beaten by the steady stream of people between the bookstore, the prospective animal center, and the offices of CDFU and the Prince William Sound Aquaculture Corporation (PWSAC — pronounced pizzwac) a couple doors down, the City Hall down around the corner where COSDRO was located, and below that the harbor where, because of the storm and the closures by then of herring, shrimp, sablefish, and crab seasons, the better part of Cordova's fishing fleet was docked against its will. The salmon season remained in doubt.

Richard had purchased the store's last navigation chart of Prince William Sound and we had it spread out between us. Richard touched the places he'd been to. I let the map emblaze itself on my mind, especially Knight Island, which had the shape of a very ornate paladin. To one side of us were windows that overlooked the harbor. Beneath us on the other side, a window faced First Street. People passed by. A clump of them had stopped and were engaged in intense conversation. One burly man in an orange coat thumped his palm with his fist as he spoke. A pickup jerked up against the curb and the driver jumped out and lurched up the sidewalk. Outside, it rained steadily, but the atmosphere on the street was electric. The rain was the tailing of the second major storm that would move the slick, during the otherwise unusual period of calm for late March and early April.

Richard said that he'd seen a blacktailed deer trapped in the crude, and a sea otter that had scratched its eyes out. He made a motion with his hands, scraping down from his eyes across his cheeks, and it was then that he said, "It tore up its own face. It scratched out its eyes because of the hydrocarbons. It died with its paws folded on its chest, where they stopped from the scratching. Another otter had chewed off a paw. There was a starfish, still alive, but half-eaten through by crude."

Richard had felt sick since he'd got back, as if he had the flu or a cold. As time went by, similar symptoms among beach crews and workers in the animal rescue centers would become the subject of dispute. Some would argue that it was the effect of the fumes. Others would say that it was merely an influenza passed among people working long hours in sometimes close quarters. I was never able to learn the truth about that, but my suspicion was that the answer was not simple. Nothing about the oil, from its chemical makeup to the manner of its mobility, and nothing about the response of stressed organisms to it, whether that of humans, animals, or vegetation, was simple. As we spoke, the slick was out there roving around in all its complication. Driven by wind and current, it was an infinitely malleable, elastic blob that could vary in thickness from a couple of feet to a hundredth of an inch. It picked up sediment and grew heavy. It coated the birds and sea otters. It was death, possibly, to the microscopic lower reaches of the food chain, and to fish. It might cancel the fishing for the year. Richard's chair creaked as he leaned back. He got a hollow look in his eyes, and said, "The place was devoid of life. Ever since I've felt a weird detachment from life."

...ON THE MORNING of the spill in Cordova, Rick Steiner, the Marine Advisory agent was awakened at 7:00 by a telephone call. He went to his office at the harbor where he worked the phone, seeking information. He also tried to get two Fish and Wildlife agents stationed in Cordova to go out and assess the spill, but they wouldn't move. Steiner then walked up the hill to the CDFU office, where he found Jack Lamb, David Grimes, Jeff Guard, and Marilyn Leland, who was still on the phone, taking calls and otherwise trying to get word on what was going to be done. She called Exxon, Alyeska, the Coast Guard, the DEC, EPA, and FWS. At 9:00 a.m., she informed Exxon that she had 30 volunteer boats ready to assist with containing the spill. At noon, she informed Alyeska that she had 75 boats, including 15 from Tatitlek. What she eventually heard from Alyeska and Exxon on Saturday was that they were "reluctant to use the boats because of the liability connected to using amateurs."

As Steiner, Grimes, Guard, and Lamb talked in the CDFU office, they were joined by other fishermen. The place was loaded with confused, worried people. Lamb pulled out the Alyeska contingency plan. It said that any spill within 50 miles of the terminal could be contained in 12 hours. The group knew a few things from the reports they were receiving: first, that the spill was much less than 50 miles from the terminal; second, that so far, eight or nine hours after the spill, nothing at all had happened; and third, that no one had any idea what was going to happen except that the spill would spread. They talked of the threat to the imminent million-dollar herring fishery, and the likely effect of a storm upon the slick. Steiner decided to take a flight out to see for himself what was going on, and he saw the same thing that Riki Ott and Chuck Monnett had seen: the spill, the Exxon *Valdez* listing on the reef, the *Baton Rouge* deballasting, and no boom, no barges, no skimmers, and nothing coming, and lumps in the oil that were sea otters, and sea lions swimming in it.

Steiner returned to Cordova and spent most of the night talking to fishermen about what they could do. Many of the fishermen had already geared up their boats to fight the spill. Steiner is a tall man, blonde, bearded, lean, pleasant, and smart. He has a way of listening closely that inspires trust, and — as his role would develop over the next year and a half — a way of maintaining effectiveness and hopefulness even in the densest tangles of power politics and litigation. He held the fishermen's respect not only for his knowledge of the sound as a biologist but also for the fact that he ran his own seiner boat. His knowledge had been trued by reality.

The next day, Steiner flew over the spill again and found that it had expanded toward Naked Island. He went on to Valdez in hopes of getting information there to pass back to Cordova. Like Riki Ott, he found chaos, the national press installed, federal scientists who had come more to monitor than to take action, the DEC completely lacking in the equipment to do anything, Exxon keeping people out of its makeshift headquarters in the Westmark Hotel, and Alyeska not answering its telephones. Steiner called his friend, David Grimes, and told him to get over to Valdez. Grimes, himself a fisherman, an accomplished musician and poet, a natural historian, and a man possessed of an uncanny ability to bring diverse people together, would become the oil spill's metaphysician.

The Cordova contingent in Valdez came to consist of Steiner, Ott, Grimes, Lamb, and Guard. Their forces were augmented by, among others, Doris Lopez, a Valdez fisherman, Ray Cesarini, a Valdez cannery operator, who provided temporary living quarters, Jim and Nancy Lethcoe, Valdez tour boat operators, historians, and activists, and Theo Mathews of Soldatna, the president of United Fishermen of Alaska. By the third day of the spill, Sunday, the twenty-sixth, the population of Valdez had almost doubled, and at a press conference that afternoon, the group heard Frank Iarossi, the head of Exxon shipping, announce that the oil spill had progressed beyond the point where it could be contained mechanically, and that plans were being formulated to use dispersants and laser-ignited burns. To the group, the news was chilling.

They stayed all Sunday night, as the first gale blew the oil slick around, and put together what Grimes referred to as the "educational press conference" in which several of them presented various subjects — fisheries, ecology, oil pollution, dispersants, local history. The press conference was held the next day. It built on the ground Riki Ott had first taken in the Exxon press conferences and resulted in wide national coverage and yet more pressure placed upon Exxon. The interests of those concerned with wildlife and fisheries had been permanently lodged as a factor in the battle. Afterwards, the DEC second-in-command, Larry Dietrich, who had been ordered by Governor Cowper to "do something," arranged with his boss, Dennis Kelso, for members of the group — Steiner, Grimes, Ott, and Lamb — to join the brass at a meeting of the oil spill triumvirate that night. Jack Lamb was the only one among the group with a family. He was by nature more conservative than the others, more patient, more given to working within regulations, and a bit uncomfortable at being cast in the role of a rabblerouser. He was the best at talking to the brass. Unassuming, clean-cut and square-jawed, Lamb looks like a high-school football coach. David Grimes would tell me later that Lamb "was brilliant, a pillar. Though he took some heat for it later back in Cordova, he became the de facto spokesman for fishermen."

At the meeting, the group found that the brass knew very little about the currents and tidal patterns of the sound. The result, thanks largely to Kelso's insistence and Iarossi's willingness to listen, was that they were heeded and, then, to their amazement, given the power to order equipment and formulate plans. Considering that the oil spill was completely out of control, they decided to focus their attention on protecting selected spawning streams, herring catchments at Knight Island's Herring Bay, and the hatchery system. David Grimes said, "When it looks like everything's lost, you're freed from limitations. You can go for it."

Back in Cordova, many of the fishermen were vacillating between blockading the tanker channel and continuing to marshal volunteer forces to fight the spill, first more or less independently of the group in Valdez, and then in tandem with it. Some, such as Tom Copeland, preferred independent action. He outfitted his boat with a pump and five-gallon buckets, then went out looking for oil. Near Knight Island, the first day they pulled out 1,500 gallons, and on their best day they drew 2,500 gallons, while Exxon's best skimmer collected just 1,200 gallons a day which raised fairly compelling questions about what might have happened if the authorities had turned the "amateurs" loose to begin with.

What came to be known as the mosquito fleet, a small armada of seiners, bowpickers, long-liners, and skiffs and the ferry *Bartlett*, commandeered by the DEC from the Alaska State Ferry System, eventually made their way to the Koernig Hatchery at Sawmill Bay on Evans Island. Despite Iarossi's initial receptivity, battles with the Exxon system continued. There were unending complications, shortfalls of equipment, and lapses in communication. Steiner would say, "The disaster was unfolding minute by minute. None of us had gone through anything like this before, so we were winging it…. The fishermen needed stronger boom, more skimmers, and better logistical support…. Exxon's people were trying, but the company was still our biggest hassle…. We'd say we needed something and they'd say, 'Yes, we've ordered it. Yes, it's on the way.' Then it took days. At first we believed them. Then we realized they were just trying to get us off their backs. There were so many people in the chain of command that if one link goofed, nothing got done." Finally, the hatcheries were saved from the main onslaught of oil, but questions of lingering damage to the salmon fry and to the hatchery grounds awaited returns from the 1989 release, which would not begin until 1991.

…"MOST FISHERMEN are fair," said Belen Cook, a slight, dark-haired woman. Belen and her husband·are gillnetters who fish for herring and salmon off Cordova in the Copper River Flats. "If they see that Exxon is fair, they may be satisfied, but Exxon has proven that not everything they say is true." Belen believed that Exxon should pay punitive damages, in addition to paying for the losses. "The unknown is frightening," she said. She said she had cried, and that she would never have dreamed of seeing the men cry that she had.

We were in the CDFU headquarters. Ken Adams came quietly out of the office at my back and sat down, took off his hat and ran his fingers slowly through his white hair. He was probably in his early forties, intense and handsome, and had emerged as yet another of the forceful CDFU spokespersons. We faced each other on the long side of a particle-board table, which was up against the wall that separated CDFU from PWSAC. Beside us was an open area and in it were more tables loaded with heaps of photocopied material — fishing closure announcements, press releases, newspaper articles. People passed in and out. Adams told me that he'd awakened in the middle of the night and had three visions. The first was of David and Goliath. "Should the people of Cordova offer Exxon terms? Did David give Goliath a chance?

"Bush should be impeached," he said. "He's pimping big oil. Are we still a free people?" This was his second vision — the wimp transformed into a pimp. Adams had a message for the boardmembers of big corporations: "I know you are good Americans, and so I personally invite you to come out on my fishing boat. I'll supply the gloves, boots, and chow. You supply the toothbrushes. Do you know what work is?"

His third vision was of covering the Exxon boardmembers with oil and letting them suffer the fate of the sea otters. "Then they would know." He glanced at my notebook as if to make sure I had that right, then added that most of what he was saying was personal, not necessarily a CDFU position. By this time, I understood a little more about what was at stake with the fishermen. I understood that Ken Adams, like many here, was caught in a terrific, mortal bind: his life, his livelihood, his home, his values, his family and friends, everything pitched against the oil slick. He was not a radical. Like Jack Lamb, he was well accustomed to working within the system.

Adams had an explanation for why it had taken so long for Alyeska and Exxon to begin cleaning up the spill: "They didn't want to clean it up. Who's accountable? Does accountability simply mean pay on the books? Exxon didn't understand responsibility. For Exxon appropriate measures mean confusion, manipulation, and deception. It's incomprehensible that they couldn't clean it up if they wanted to. We had phenomenally good weather until yesterday — day seventeen of the spill. Exxon can't say the weather made it impossible to clean it up. They were counting on bad weather to use as an excuse and they didn't get it."

It made sense. It was the same principle as running tankers until they broke down, of using a faulty delivery system. It was cheaper to keep things that way and sidetrack the regulators. Similarly, it was cheaper to figure that the spill wouldn't happen, and if it did, then to wait for the wind to come up, to hang tight and try to control the imagery. When I asked Exxon representatives about this later, they denied it, even exhibited outrage at such a suggestion, but an examination of the events as they occurred — the lack of preparation, the indecision, the confusion, the footdragging, the impediments, the refusal to consult the knowledgeable until pushed into it — lent credence to Adams's accusation.

Author's Note. As it happened, the salmon returns of 1991 referred to above (as well as the returns of 1990) came in record breaking numbers. Exxon promoted this in national advertisements as evidence of the success of its cleanup, but what it really attested to was the inventiveness and resolve of the volunteer fleet of fishing vessels that protected the hatcheries. The wild salmon runs, which went unprotected in the early stages of the spill, and which are critical to maintaining the genetic diversity of hatchery runs, were severely affected.

MAGADAN LUCK

MAGADAN OBLAST, the Soviet Far East, a far-flung corner of the Russian Republic, beyond even Siberia.

We met our Russian counterparts, scientists with the Institute of Biological Problems of the North. One studied the plankton in lakes, another the population cycles of lemmings, still others the successions and distributions of plants.

"And what is your specialty?" they asked.

Our interpreter helped me with "She works for senators," but that brought only puzzled looks. I pantomimed catching fish with a rod and reel, laid my hands — fingers splayed — across one another to look like web.

"Ah! *Ribachka!*" Their eyes lit up. We would go fishing!

The idea of the "expedition" of Alaskans to the Soviet Far East was that we would join with counterparts to work on biological or environmental problems. As an environmentalist and a recent assistant to the Alaska legislature on natural resource issues, I'd anticipated a cooperative effort to plant seedlings or haul tires out of a trashed river. My interest in the trip was based mostly, however, on a long-time fascination with this mysterious northern land to our west, and I wanted to be there, to see for myself the country that's been called Alaska's divided twin.

When I packed my duffel bag for Magadan, I threw in a lightweight spinning rod that had come in the mail one day, a bonus for buying a new outboard. Though I know something about fish, I don't often meet them on the end of a line. In Alaska, I fish commercially for salmon, gillnetting them in beach sets; my idea of fishing is standing knee-deep in sockeyes, snapping web from gill, the muscles in my hands aching. In my circles, to "fly fish" means to load salmon into an airplane and haul them to a processor.

The helicopter landed on a sandbar. The Alaskan and Russian botanists, a black dog the size of a bear and I disembarked into clouds of mosquitoes. We were in the Magadan Reserve, one of the Soviet Union's system of natural areas set aside for preservation and scientific study. A broad, slow-moving river flowed through a landscape of stubby black spruce and birch forests leading into low, purple hills. Several small buildings — the reserve's headquarters, home to its guardian rangers — were half-hidden in the trees, just up from the river bank.

There were more than enough hands to help with dinner, so I took my rod down to the river, tied on a Mepps lure and made some casts. The river was too shallow adjacent to the sandbar, so I walked upstream to where the bank fell off more sharply. The mosquitoes weren't any worse than in interior Alaska, which is not to say that they weren't among the worst in the world.

Vladimir, one of our hosts from the institute, appeared on the bank, sucking on a cigarette. He spoke to me in Russian, none of which I understood, wrinkled his nose, waved derisively with his hand, pointed at my rod, frowned. Translation: This wasn't a good fishing place, and my equipment was totally unsuitable.

For dinner, served at an outdoor table balanced on logs, we had fishhead soup. Gamely, our uninitiated Americans sipped broth from around the staring salmon eyes, the white globs of milt and the legions of kamikaze mosquitoes that dove into their bowls.

After the hours-long dinner, after the speeches and toasts and the exhausting efforts at politeness and communication, I was ready for my sleeping bag. Our interpreter called me over. "You're going fishing," he said. Vladimir was nodding. So was a man who looked like he'd just stepped out of a jungle; he was wearing a mosquito-net hat, the net tied up away from his face; a dirt-colored heavy-duty field suit with a huge knife on the belt; and several days' beard. This was Boris, assistant ranger. Boris pointed downriver. Just over there, we would go, just for a little while, we would definitely catch some fish.

I didn't seem to have a choice. I recruited Debby, one of our botanists, and we zoomed off in a powerboat with Boris and Vladimir.

This far north, early in July, there was plenty of light at ten-thirty. The sky was stretched with cirrus clouds, high and feathery and lit from below with pale pink edges. The river washed past snags of fallen trees and banks overgrown with grasses. Debby peered into the foliage, recognizing a lupine, a spirea. We rounded one bend and another and then pulled up beside a side slough.

Fish waggled in the bottom of the pool. I hadn't known what we were to fish for, but I recognized these by their sail-sized dorsals. We traded our names for them — *kharioos*, grayling — as we readied our poles. Vladimir had a spinning rod with a big, shiny spoon. Boris had the world's largest fly rod, nearly as thick as my wrist at its base, long enough to reach across the slough. Boris looked at my rod and, frowning, said something to Vladimir. His tone was disparaging.

I cast into the pool. On my second cast, a fish swept forward and took the lure.

Boris leaned his own pole into the bushes and ran to help me. Shouting excitedly, he grabbed my line and began to pull it in, fast, hand over hand. Debby and I looked at each other. "Must be the Russian way," I said. Boris yanked the fish up onto the bank, unhooked it and slid a stringer through its gills. It was a nice fish, perhaps fifteen inches long, its scales like rows of silver buttons. We all enthused over it, and Boris and Vladimir took up their poles again with a new intensity. I handed mine to Debby.

Debby caught a fish, and then I caught one. Debby yelled, "*Nyet! nyet!*" and wouldn't let Boris grab the line. "*Americanski* way," we told him and showed what it was like to let the fish take off, to dive and fight and flash and be reeled back in. Boris looked worried and then amazed when I landed the played-out fish on my own. He stretched his rod across the slough and dropped his fly near the opposite bank. Vladimir, farther along, cast and cast again; his reel zinged as he cranked the line in.

Debby caught another.

Boris suddenly became very interested in my rod. He ran his hand over it, testing the flex, pinching the line. He held the lure in the air and let it twist, glinting, back and forth. He mumbled in Russian. "Try it," I said, pushing the rod at him, but he wouldn't take it.

"Vladimir," I said, "try this." I gave him one of my Mepps. He put it in his tackle box. I gave Boris a Mepps, too, and he dropped it into a jar with his homemade flies.

I cast again, caught and played and landed another grayling.

The men exchanged looks. Neither had hooked anything yet.

We heard the sound of another boat. It was Sergei, the head ranger, and two others of our party, fresh from the sauna. They admired our

29

catch as we all swatted mosquitoes. Boris began to take his pole apart. He had an idea. He was going to get his net.

While he zipped back to the camp, the rest of us took the other boat around a couple of more curves to the river's juncture with a side creek. In the creek mouth, we could see where salmon-sized fish were finning, breaking the water into silvery rifts that reflected the remaining light. I flung my lure at them a few times, but it was too dark to hope for more than an accidental snagging. Sergei boiled water on a campstove and served jam "tea" — a spoonful of jam stirred into a mug of hot water.

Boris returned with a pile of tangled gill net. I helped him work through the net, laying it out on the boat's bow — the line with cork floats to one side, the line with metal rings to the other, the web picked free of sticks in the center. "I do this in Alaska," I said. "Five species" — I held up five fingers — "in Alaska."

"*Keta*," Boris said, and I understood. The chum or dog salmon, the one with striped sides — its scientific name is *keta*. I spread my fingers again and made vertical stripes in the air. Boris grinned. We were talking about the same fish.

When the net was laid out neatly, we tied one end to shore where the creek merged with the river's slower water. We pushed the boat backward into the current with an oar, and the net spilled off the bow to lie in a line. We waited, and Boris described what a big splash we would see when a fish hit the net. The fish, though, weren't moving, or they weren't crossing the current, and so we left the net and motored back to camp.

In the morning, we had five *keta* salmon to add to our mess of grayling. Vladimir and I cleaned them. He used my dictionary to tell me that he respected a woman who cleaned fish.

A thousand miles to the northeast of Magadan Reserve, our three powerboats headed upriver, startling moose, reindeer, swans, geese, loons, hares — a richer collection of animals than I'd ever seen in one place. I'd left the botanists and joined another group of Alaskans to fly to the Soviet arctic, to a scientific station on the coastal plain. The scientists here specialized in parasites. None of us knew anything about parasites, but we'd been happy to hike up a mountain, set vole traps on the tundra and eat reindeer stew. Now, our hosts were taking us fishing.

We wound back and forth along the ribbon of river. The mountain we'd climbed previously was sometimes in front of us, sometimes to our right, sometimes behind us. Now and then the lead boat missed the channel and ground up a cloud of river bottom with its prop. I watched the banks; where the river cut into them, it exposed a wall of ice beneath the sod. I was hoping to spot a tusk or a frozen, fleshy leg of a mammoth. In the geological museum in Magadan, we'd seen a cast of a whole baby mammoth that was found in permafrost near here.

Someone pointed. A leggy, flag-tailed, blond and copper-colored fox was racing along the shore. For a second, it seemed as though the animal and we were part of the same stopped action, and that it was the backdrop land that was moving past us. And then the fox was up over the bank and gone.

There were buildings ahead, wooden skiffs pulled up on the beach. We slowed and turned in. A couple of men came out of one of the cabins and watched us from behind a length of gill net that was hung, like a fence, in front of the camp. Wooden barrels were piled to one side.

I reached for my fishing pole, but Valeriy, the chief Soviet parasitologist, stopped me. Not yet. This was, apparently, just a visit stop. Wilhelm, one of our drivers, knew the men here. They were preparing for the run of arctic char that would come later in the summer.

The men were dark, chain-smoking and shy. Wilhelm talked to them while the rest of us stood around awkwardly. I looked into a barrel. It was stuck with lumpy, gray salt and smelled like fish. I looked at the gill net, fingering the web, lifting the lead line. I assumed the net was stretched out for mending, which it needed, but I couldn't find where it had been mended, ever, nor any sign of needle and twine.

The men — Americans, too — had disappeared into one of the cabins. I found them passing around and admiring hunting rifles. A pile of unloaded bullets lay on the nearest bed, sunk into the folds of a faded blue sleeping bag. An electric lightbulb dangled from the center of the ceiling, and the most prominent object in the room was a large television set. I had to look longer to find the net-mending needle, burnished wood, on a nail by the door.

It was time to go. We piled back into the boats and continued upriver, running aground with greater frequency, until we came to a wide curve in the river, a long gravelly beach where we anchored.

The morning's clouds had broken up into scraps of gray fleece, uncovering an ice-blue sky. The sun was almost directly overhead, and there was no shade anywhere. Valeriy pointed at the portion of the river that swept around the curve, indicating that was where we should fish, but the water there looked too fast to me. I took my rod and cut across the top of the beach, through a sandy area where dense, thin-leaved plants were so thickly covered with pink blossoms they looked like bouquets stuck in the sand. I brushed past willow bushes, setting loose an air show of white fluff. The bank on the far side fell off sharply into a deep pool.

Kharioos. I could see half a dozen grayling, all good-sized, all lying on the bottom against the shore. They were finning as though fanning themselves, using as little energy as possible. Clearly, they were not in a mood for feeding.

I cast across the pool and watched my Mepps flash its way back, looking like nothing that might occur naturally in the river. It nearly ran into one fish, which turned to look at it and then, slowly, eased back into position.

I fished for an hour like that, annoying one fish and then another, but never enough to coax them into a hit.

To tell the truth, I didn't mind about the fish. I felt the sun on my face and the arctic breeze, and I listened to the water. I cast and cast again, and it was the motion that mattered — mindless, repetitive, rhythmic. I though about Norman Maclean, the fisherman-writer whose father had used a metronome to teach him to fish, to melt into the rhythms of the universe.

My mosquito lotion wore off all at once, and, until I stopped to slather more on, I understood the panic of Alaska's caribou and Russia's reindeer, animals that sometimes get driven by mosquitoes to exhausted deaths.

Back down the river, I could see the others, spaced apart, casting into faster water, Valeriy with this thick wool hat piled on his head like a turban. I mentally pinched myself. I was in the Soviet arctic, fishing with Russians for Russian fish. How could I ever have imagined, growing up through all those years of anticommunism and Cold War fear, that this was possible? Here we were, Russians and Americans together, sharing the same universal rhythms, in what must be one of the wildest and most sparely beautiful, not to mention peaceful, places on our shrinking earth.

I worked my way toward the others, testing the faster water. When I reached Valeriy, he told me, in his fractured English, that he liked that I liked to fish and that he was impressed with American women. We — the three here at Ust-Chaun — were the first he'd ever met. I understood him to say that we did everything that Soviet women did and more, and I was embarrassed. I didn't think Soviet women had time for such idleness as fishing; they were all too busy, working double-duty at their paid jobs and their domestic ones — the long hours of shopping for short supplies, preparing meals from scratch, homemaking without the labor-saving equipment Americans take for granted. Even here, among scientists posted to a remote research station, women were cooking, caring for children, attending to chores.

At that moment, from a clearing near where the boats were anchored, Luda called us to tea. She had spread a picnic cloth on the ground and was slicing cucumbers. I carved a loaf of bread on our boat bow. The others trailed in. No one had caught any fish, no one complained, everyone plucked par-boiled mosquitoes from their cups of tea. I practiced my Russian. *Komar.* Mosquito. Across the river a swan, its wings walloping the air with a sound like towels being snapped in the wind, launched itself, circled over us and headed east.

We went back to fish some more. Luda stayed by the boats; she did not care to fish, she said.

The sun had fallen considerably, and my fishing hole was now partially shaded by the bank. I heard the fish before I even came around the corner. They were rising through the shade, snatching at mosquitoes, leaving widening rings that merged one into another. They weren't jumping, just snouting through the surface, then falling back again. I cast into the pool, repeatedly. Now and then, a fish would make a run at my Mepps before veering off. I thought of Boris, back at Magadan Reserve, how much he'd love to be here with his giant fly rod. When we left the reserve, I'd told him that when he came to Alaska, I would be *his* fishing guide. It had been the wrong thing to say, of course. We both knew his chances of ever coming to Alaska were close to zero. His chances of dropping a line in his own arctic were probably similar.

33

And I thought again what I had thought a thousand times since arriving in the Magadan region — what right do Americans have, by the accident of their birth on one soil instead of another, to such enormous privilege?

I thought this like a mantra — what right, what right — and I listened to the river. Along the shore, it made a whispery noise, like rough cotton rubbing against itself. Farther out, it rustled around rocks with a silkier sound. After a while, I could hear single pieces of gravel washing past each other, but I still had no answer to my questions.

By then, I had sufficiently annoyed the pool of fish that one retaliated by striking my lure. We struggled with one another, back and forth along the bank, until I landed it, gills heaving, in the sand. I fished some more, and I had another. I hooked another and lost it. I caught a third, one so small I would have released it had I not hooked it so well.

I saw Wilhelm crossing a channel farther upstream, and then the others, everyone circling back to the boats. It was all I could do to break away, to reel in and not to cast again, to pick up my fish and leave my piece of river.

Back at the boats, we showed off our fish. With three, I was the highliner again. Wilhelm, fly fishing, had caught only one. He flashed a huge, gold-toothed smile at me.

"You are happy," Luda said.

Yes, I was, and I also knew that was not exactly what she'd meant to say. The Russian language has a single word for both happiness and luck. If you're lucky, you must also be happy. If you're happy, it's not that you have some constitutional guarantee, some inalienable right to be so, but only that you have enjoyed good luck.

"*Ochen*," I said. Very.

34

WEIGHT

BY ROBERT STUBBLEFIELD

AS A CHILD, I accompanied my father, grandfather, and older brother on fishing and hunting trips to Cottonwood Creek, Middle Fork Junction, and Windy Canyon. People I loved and places I came to love were more important than limiting out or filling tags.

A decade later, when I began fishing and hunting myself, success became a matter of weight: a heavy wicker creel layered with rainbow trout and sedgegrass, chukar partridge sagging the pocket of my game vest, and the heft of a field-dressed mule deer on a hemp rope strung over a limb of the black locust planted by my grandmother. Carrying that weight home, first to my parents' house, and then my own, was the essence of fishing and hunting.

My mother believes your life is presented to you as you are able to accept it. Although daily surrounded by people and events proving otherwise, I become more inclined to believe her with time. Perhaps our lives are always at our core, only presenting themselves as we become perceptive enough to recognize.

If we are fortunate enough to live a life recognizable from a distance as our own, it is impossible to forget the stimulus. For me, the stimulus was a day of fishing which left me aware it was time to start leaving weight behind, to begin peeling back layers obscuring truths once inherent.

My friend Bill and I arrived on Cottonwood Creek late in the afternoon on that last Sunday of October in 1987. I parked my '63 Chevy pickup about a hundred yards above the creek, where a summer thunderstorm had washed out the road.

Through August and most of September, I'd worked the peppermint harvest seven days a week, all the while stealing frequent, longing glances at the North Fork of the John Day River. Afterward, four cord of firewood kept me off the trout streams. I was anxious; and when we made the creek I casted as if determined to cram two months of lost fishing into one evening.

Flyfishing was new to me; I made errors of judgement and execution which I was aware of, plus myriad others of which I was unaware. I had strikes, but was either too fast or too slow on the hits I recognized. I wanted that first fish in my creel, and my impatience cost me.

Bill fished downstream and was getting steady action, either playing a fish or kneeling to release one every time I looked. He was the best fly-fisherman I knew, and I tried to emulate his casting technique, but my bullwhip casts weren't easily discarded. Remembering that Bill had tied on a black ant before we parted, I switched the grey elk-hair caddis I had on to a black ant from my own box.

Halfway to the hole where I had told Bill I would turn back, I was yet to land a fish. The canvas creel swung uselessly from my side. I wanted weight in it; a fat trout to thump reassuringly against my ribs.

Small stream fishing requires a short leader and a delicate touch. I knew I scared away more fish than ever saw my fly land. Despite my awkwardness, the first fish finally came. As soon as I landed the nine-inch rainbow, I struck its head on a rock and put it on the layer of grass at the bottom of my creel. I killed the fish quickly and thoughtlessly, without consideration. As a child of children of the depression, releasing legal-size fish was not my first instinct.

Leaning my rod against the cutbank, I put my hands into the water to wash them. Kneeling down, close to water and soil, I smelled the fertile odor of good trout water mixed with falling and fallen leaves, forming a dusky smell that reminded me this was a place where plants and animals had been living, breeding, and dying since the creek started cutting this canyon, since before it carved through the stubborn basalt and layers of easily erodible John Day Formation ash which turn the water brick red each spring.

October of 1987 marked the twentieth year since my grandfather's death, and when I resumed fishing I stood farther back from the holes and tried to fish with the economy and patience I remembered in his methodic fishing of these very waters. I considered each stretch of water and determined a casting strategy before moving on it.

The shadow from the western rim of the canyon had crossed the creek and engulfed me. I didn't have much fishing time left. Fall twilights are short along creek bottoms.

Yellow leaves from namesake cottonwood trees fell and drifted on the current, some catching in eddies along the side. Clean weather could hold weeks, but the next strong winds would pull along slate-grey storm clouds from the gulf of Alaska. 'Wind doesn't blow after the first of November for the hell of it' I'd heard old-timers say.

According to the Boyer's Cash Store thermometer on my front porch, it had been sixty-five degrees when I left the house. Already it was chilly enough that I wished I'd worn waders instead of jeans and canvas basketball shoes. After fishing, I knew I'd stand wet and cold in gathering darkness for a moment, feeling a trace of winter before starting for the warm house I shared with my wife, where she would have a salad made, and herbs cut to sprinkle on the fish, but also a pound of hamburger thawed just in case.

Sidecasting to keep under the willows and brush along the bank, I worked up the riffles to where the creek made a ninety-degree bend. I took several small fish from the riffles, but released them.

The cliff hole, about fifty yards above the bend, marked the point where I'd told Bill I'd turn around. When I was a small boy fishing with my family, the cliff hole was the upstream boundary of fishable territory for my grandfather and me. Broad, gravel-lined banks gave way to a narrow gorge above. The hole at the bottom was left like a plum for us, although I'm certain my brother occasionally tried it as he leapfrogged ahead to rougher country upstream.

The water was shallow on the side next to me, but ran deeper against the twenty foot cliff along the other side.

I approached the pool quietly, but not quietly enough to avoid alarming the swallows in their nests at the upper part of the rock face. Keeping my distance and attempting to remain far enough away to avoid spooking fish, I false-casted and worked out line to reach the head of the pool.

My first cast fell short and drifted toward the middle of the stream where a fish rose and bumped it, then turned away. The second and third casts were better, but still not the cast to land the fly gently at the top of the hole and drift it over the black water at the undercut base of the rock.

Moving to within my casting range risked spooking the fish upstream, or at least enough to prevent them from rising. In flyfishing, the degree of luck involved to land a fish is inversely proportional to its size, and at that point in my apprenticeship, blind luck was all I had to rely on.

Whether movement or shadow betrayed him, or whether I managed to hear his steps over the sound of moving water I'm not sure, but I became aware of Bill watching my efforts from behind. I didn't have to turn to know he was there. I imagine he was trying to decide between making his presence known or creeping downstream without letting on having watched over my clumsy efforts.

Saving him the decision, I turned toward him and shrugged my shoulders. Bill stood on the bank with one foot slightly ahead of the other, his denim pants dark and wet to the top of his thighs. And although Bill actually looks very little like my grandfather, at that moment, at least to me, he appeared remarkably similar. Both men were small and wiry, with an aura of capability about them.

Up until the last few years I had worn clothes from my grandfather's trunk, until finally outgrowing even his oversize carpenter pants. A thought as abstract as the fact that Bill was a man who would fit my grandfather's clothes triggered a vision of what would happen next as tangible and certain as the rock face of the cliff — Bill and I would change positions and he would fish the hole as it was meant to be fished. And that is what happened.

I told Bill I didn't believe I could make the cast from where I stood. He agreed I would have to advance too close to the hole in order to put my fly where it needed to go. And just as it did not trouble me that Bill had quite likely been taking fish from water behind me, it did not bother me to defer to him on this of all holes.

His first cast landed where the best of my efforts had, about two feet short of where he wanted. But in his case the perfect cast was an inevitability rather than a possibility. Somehow it reassured me that he casted for the same spot I had. The next cast landed on a dish of quiet water where the black ant sat, then swirled and was taken by the current.

The only part I later regretted was looking away from the fly toward Bill, and that instant missing the fish thrust out of that dark water and take the fly. I saw Bill twitch his rod tip and set the hook, then switch his rod to his left hand and strip out line with the right.

The trout started upstream, then turned and dove back toward the rock. Bill kept sideways pressure on it, attempting to work it into slower water on our side of the creek. He reeled line in, then gave some back as the fish veered toward the middle of the stream.

Bill and the fish were dance partners; first one leading, then the other. I saw the glint of the trout turning on its side. Bill called for me to get in position to net it, then pulled it toward me by backing up as I reached out.

The trout arched double from its own weight as I scooped it into my net. I grabbed my pliers and twisted the hook from its bottom lip, then lowered it back into the water, removed the net, and cupped my hands beneath it. I faced the fish upstream and worked it gently back and forth in the current. Exhausted and slow to respond, the fish finally began to work its gills.

Water no longer flowed around me as I knelt in the current, but through me. And rather than being clear, it was amber and sustentative, containing the color of leaf, tree, sky, and rock. The trout seemed to have gathered all that color into its body and exploded into an incandescent mottle of spots and stripes containing black night, brown earth, red blood, and promised blue of long-ago sky.

The fish breathed, and I slowly removed my hands from underneath it, expecting the temporary holding, then the quick dart that would carry it away. Instead, the trout held for a brief moment, then rolled in the slight current. And all that glorious color gave way to the stark, white underbelly marking death and submission.

I reached for the fish. My limited experience had yet to diminish my ego enough to believe something could die as I held it and willed it to live.

The weight of the fish in my hand felt like weight to leave behind, a layer of the surface obscuring part of me ready to be exposed. As if realizing my stubborn naivety, the fish began to work its gills again. It flicked its tail, and as I removed my hands, swam first two feet upstream, hesitated, then turned and disappeared toward the rock.

I stood and let the water run off me, in that moment knowing I would never again take on the weight of killing without thought. I waded out onto the gravel toward Bill, then we climbed the bank and followed a game trail downstream toward the truck.

It is impossible to avoid tempering recollection of that day with what was to follow. Eventually, memories become impossible to separate, and we ultimately abandon guarding the gates between.

But even then I felt a sense of finality which transcended the closing weekend of fishing season. As I walked through the semi-darkness with Bill, it was impossible for me to know that by the following September his marriage would break apart in a way frightening and painful even to witness, impossible to know that optimism for the life we were leading would erode enough to cause my wife and me to pack our possessions into my brother-in-law's truck and move to Portland, and later feel elation in having mutually escaped an unexplored life by the barest margins.

I was a very young man at that point, and it seemed I had existed on the periphery of my own life for too long, and that it was time to begin edging closer to the core.

AN INTERVIEW WITH WILLIAM KITTREDGE

FROM ...WHEN WE TALK ABOUT RAYMOND CARVER

INTERVIEWED BY SAM HALPERT

SAM HALPERT: You and Ray were good friends. When did you first meet him?

WILLIAM KITTREDGE: Well, it's real clear. I can be specific because I remember it so vividly. It was during spring break 1970, I was teaching at the University of Montana, and the woman who was my wife at that time and I went to Seattle, you know, just to get out of Montana and hang around for a while at the Olympic, one of the old grand hotels. They were having one of those college English teachers' conventions there, whatever the acronym is. The place was pretty near empty. I don't remember what the meeting was about, but it was something like nine o'clock at night, and they had these long bookstalls with all the publishers' books lined up — maybe two hundred yards of bookstalls and nobody around at all. The place is empty and I'm walking around and looking at these books and trying to resist the impulse to heist a couple of them. My wife and I and a guy way down at the far end were the only ones around. Anyway, I picked up a copy of a book edited by Curt Johnson, who, incidentally, was the publisher of the journal where "Will You Please Be Quiet, Please?" first appeared. I was browsing through the book when this guy walks up. He's kind of a scruffy-looking guy, looks over my shoulder and says, "I've got a story in there." My first impulse was to say something like, "Yeah, I'll bet you have." In any event, we kind of jousted about for a minute or two, and then it turned out it was Ray. I couldn't believe that anyone would claim that story if it weren't really theirs. So then we started talking, and he told me he had read a couple stories that I had written, which made him one of the few people in the world I had met that had ever laid eyes on a story of mine. Then we had some coffee and talked some more and someone said, "Let's have a beer." So we went to the bar and someone said, "Let's have a drink." Next thing I know we're just plastered.

Lenny Michaels told me about Ray saying that whenever he was out on that boat of his, he couldn't help wondering why the hell he wasn't home writing — where he belonged.

Oh, yes, he could be more ironic than that. He'd look at me once in a while and say, "Are we getting away with it or what?" Something like that. Like, "Look at me, here I am, a guy with a boat!" At the same time, he was very attached to it. He loved having all those things. One of the last times I saw him was in Seattle, almost at the same place where we first met. This was before he got sick. It was at a celebration for Dick Hugo about November '87. Ray and Tess were staying at a posh hotel near the Market, and Ray was talking about why didn't he and I get together and buy a condo near the Market overlooking the harbor in Seattle and so forth. I don't know where the hell he thought I'd get the money for it, but he was clearly enjoying his success at the time — embracing and having fun with it — on the other hand, not taking it too seriously. He was never obnoxious about it.

But you knew he was enjoying every minute of it?

Oh, yes. Why wouldn't he? After all, he was a saw filer's son from Yakima, and he worked hard, and all these things finally came to him. He got them by himself.

Earlier, you mentioned that "Where I'm Calling From" is largely autobiographical. Of course, that could be said of almost all of Ray's stories, and he received a few knocks for that. Could you comment on that?

42

I believe that every writer discovers the story that's theirs in a way. For a long time, the story that Ray discovered — early on, I think "A Student's Life" was the first one of any consequence — was Ray and Maryann, Ray and Maryann for a long time. One of the things his friends knew and could point out from story to story to story — and

Ray was perfectly willing to tell you — was this is the thing that happened, this is where he got that story.

She was not his only source, was she?

No, not the only. I remember Ray and I sitting at a bar in Missoula when a woman bartender told us about being arrested the night before, because she and her boyfriend got stoned and moved all their furniture out on the lawn — set up lights and all. After a while the neighbors got annoyed and called the cops. I looked at Ray and told him that had to be his. So he wrote it — changed it a little. The one about the guy moving all his stuff out in the driveway for a yard sale?

"Shall We Dance?"

Yeah, years later. But mostly he found stories in his life. Then in the transition, when he was quitting the booze, I don't know, because I wasn't with him in the sense of seeing him all the time; I don't know where those stories came from. Like "Cathedral," which I presume came from experiences he and Tess had.

Yes. Tess once worked with a blind man in Seattle.

Seems like it. So he continued to use autobiographical material. I think he had very clear standards that he learned very early on. One of the books I remember in his library in the house in Cupertino was marked up, scribbled all over. It was a college textbook on double stories. You know, Dostoevsky's story "The Double" and that story by Henry James, and all those doppelganger stories. There was a book he had used in college, maybe in a class with John Gardner. One of the things that struck me about those stories was the way they were like Ray's. Sort of put yourself in my shoes or try my blindness. They were stories that encouraged you to somehow put yourself in someone else's situation imaginatively and thereby generate compassion for them. I believe Ray formed these ideas about storytelling from the very start, way back at Chico State.

In one of Ray's later stories, "Intimacy," he depicts a writer who shares many of the feelings you have just described. This fictional writer visits his ex-wife ostensibly to seek forgiveness. How do you view that story?

Of course you never know, but I'd have to say it's a depiction of part of his feelings at least. Ray felt terrific guilt and sorrow, and he felt something valuable had been lost. He also felt that in the nature of their compact, he was the one who had walked away with all the skills — like two people in a contract, and one gets to leave with all the success and the other gets to stand out in the rain. And in a way that is what happened, and Ray felt — as anybody would — great guilt over it. Though I must say I never heard him talk about it in that way; but we both understood it wasn't a thing we *would* talk about.

Is it then possible that "Intimacy" was sort of a payback for Maryann? Perhaps Ray's way of acknowledging his debt to her?

Maybe. It's possible. Of course, you never knew with Ray. In the early days he'd used her so ruthlessly in those stories, and so maybe this was just his way of getting another story. Or maybe it was his way of paying back — probably some of both, for all we know. I don't think it was, "I'm going to make you a gift of this story." Again, I think he took his own guilt, his own life, his own deepest feelings and used them to make art out of it in ways that were partly a payment back to Maryann and at the same time another story.

What do you think of his later work?

Well, that story "Intimacy" that we were talking about — I don't know; I'm not sold on that story. I thought "Where I'm Calling From" a great story. I really loved "Errand," about the death of Chekhov. And this may be an aside from your question, but I think Ray was very deliberately changing his art when he died. That's the reason for all those poems. I think that's the reason he was recharging, exploring, looking for new directions. He had explored the old orientation as far as he wanted to. I think he was, as a major artist will, trying to enlarge his scope onto a larger stage. He was feeling his way, and these were all kind of studies toward what he'd begin to do had he not died.

He described how he loved to revise his stories, even those you've mentioned as his best pieces.

I think those longer versions of those stories of his, like "A Small, Good Thing" were really his masterworks. There is a significant difference in the stories as they appeared in *What We Talk About When We Talk About Love* and later versions. For instance, William Abrams, in his introduction to the O. Henry collection in which "A Small, Good Thing" was the leading story, said something like, wasn't it courageous of Ray to take a brief story from his previous book and enlarge it this way? Well, the fact is it was just the opposite. He had written the story, but his editor Gordon Lish had cut it down to the short version. The short version of that story is enormously diminished in its emotional power. It's no coincidence that Ray changed contractual agreements, changed editors and all that. As he told me afterward, "They can't change a comma from now on."

What's your reaction to all this talk of minimalism?

You know, I took grave exception to, for instance, people like Madison Smartt Bell attacking Ray for so-called minimalism. It's very easy to go at somebody's weaker stories and to find fault with them, which is what I believe Bell's essay did. A writer should be judged on his best work; that other stuff is forgettable. It's gone and we shouldn't waste time worrying about it.

Would you say he was not a minimalist?

I don't think of Ray in terms of being minimalist. I don't think he was an emotional minimalist at all. He was dealing with what were, at least for me, major emotions. When I reflect and see my own life in the mirror of some of those great stories, like at the end of "A Small, Good Thing," these stories are consistently telling me that I must learn to be good, to be humane, compassionate, considerate of other people. That is a major emotional orientation, and I think it's utterly important to say, absolutely political. I think Ray had a very sure sense of his politics. He was simply saying we must be more compassionate, we have to be more considerate of each other. Ray said that over and over again in major ways in all those stories.

DUWAMISH

BY R. P. JONES

I

You left us Friday and our weather changed
from morning skies still silver from the rain
to fade back down into a cold wet gray
you celebrate by calling its old name.

I walk your childhood river in that light,
past broken bottles scattered on the banks
where oil and mud and shining seepage mix
on tidal currents sliding in and out.

The river pulses slowly near the sea
as twice each day those bitter tides come in,
and twice each day the run-off drags them out
down through the reach to dump them in the bay.

You name this river with its ancient name —
Duwamish — call it gray not green,
and watch the winter waters come and go
as if they never knew which way was home.

II

You always loved the things that called us back:
water — thin rivers running from their source
down to their origin, the open sea,
by following the hollows of the land.

And rocks — the solid granite, dark basalt,
the glacial heavings pulled down to the flats
to rest at last in mud along the banks,
the soft earth sucked out on the tides as silt.

You fought your heavy way through that old mire
we all come from; you never could forget
the rocks and vacant lots, the childhood friends,
and that old church you never set foot in.

All your best pictures are in black and white,
and need a careful eye to call their shades
of gray by name and know the ones to love,
to see, in all the shadows, one called home.

III

I stop to watch a shadow swimming past
beneath the surface where this weather ends
today; I see it hesitate and turn
away on some cold current I can't feel.

What did you dream of when the last rains fell?
Another sunrise shining somewhere else?
The ebb and flow of this old tidal reach?
Or resting in your final rippling stream?

Up river aging salmon roll among
the rocks and fin themselves across old pools,
the shallow spawning waters of their birth,
the one last place they fight back to to die.

You found your own way back to this old stream
where weather turns around with every wind;
but some sure instinct must have called you here,
whichever way you went was always home.

IV

The old ones buried here once called themselves
Duwampsh — the people living on water;
they used to dance the rhythms of the Sound
and praise all moving waters to the moon.

They used to call the salmon in the fall
and sing for tides to bring them up the reach,
and rains to raise the river bringing down
the ancient messages to guide them back.

You said you came out here to walk the past,
to leave first flowers on a faded grave
for no sake but your own, and take one last
slow look around the street where you were born.

You came back here to see if anyone
still cared enough to watch the coho run
this common narrow reach down from the bay —
this was your home, this final brilliant gray.

48

THE RIVER PEOPLE PHOTOGRAPHS

BY JACQUELINE MOREAU

MY PHOTOGRAPHS of mid-Columbia River Native Americans are like scratches on a hard surface. They reveal just a glimpse of an old way of life governed by a wealth of unwritten laws and values. It is a culture struggling for due recognition, especially when interfacing with the non-Indian world.

As tribal members of the Yakima, Warm Springs, Umatilla, and Nez Perce nations reclaim their aboriginal roles as co-managers of Columbia River fish runs, many non-Indians attain greater awareness and respect for their presence. In the lives of these Indians salmon has major cultural, economic, and religious significance.

The late David Sohappy and his wife Myra symbolize past, current, and future struggles of Columbia River Indians. They have been part of three decades of successful fishing rights litigations.

In 1982, Sohappy and thirteen other river Indians were incarcerated for challenging state, federal, and tribal fishing regulations in the "Salmon Scam" undercover operation. The Indians' struggle to retain their fishing rights continues.

The photos:

Page 50: *The Klickitat and Columbia Rivers. Lyle, Washington 1988*
Page 51: *David & Myra Sohappy with a grandson, Dustin Wyena. Cook, Washington 1985*
Page 52: *David Sohappy mending fish nets. Cook, Washington 1985*
Page 53: *Fish buyer for Indian caught fish. Towal, Washington 1988*
Page 54: *David Sohappy arrested by Yakima Nation tribal police. Toppenish, Washington 1986*
Page 55: *Funeral of David Sohappy. White Swan, Washington 1991*

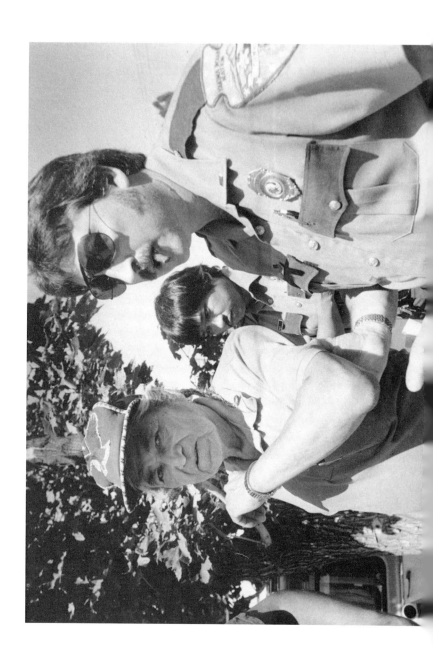

55

Fishing boats impounded by the Royal Canadian Navy at Annieville Dyke on the Fraser River, 1941. In all, about 1,200 boats were seized and sold by order in council during January–February 1942. Photo: Vancouver Public Library

JUSTICE IN OUR TIME

BY ROY MIKI AND CASSANDRA KOBAYASHI

THE UPROOTING of Japanese Canadians begun in 1942 was not an isolated act of racism, but the culmination of discriminatory attitudes directed towards them from the early days of settlement. The war itself offered the opportune moment for many powerful politicians, business and labour groups, and individuals in BC, to attack the social and economic base of the thriving Japanese Canadian community, under the guise of national security. Indeed, for many decades before, Japanese Canadians, as well as Chinese and Indo-Canadians, had been constantly harassed by many racists in BC. Older Japanese Canadians remembered well the Vancouver riot of September 7, 1907, when a crowd at an anti-Asian rally suddenly turned into a mob, stormed through Chinatown breaking store windows, and were finally beaten back at Powell Street by a group of Japanese Canadians.

Before the uprooting, over 95% of Japanese Canadians lived in BC. During the sixty-five years since the first settler from Japan, Manzo Nagano, came to Canada in 1877, legal restrictions in BC not only disenfranchised Japanese Canadians, but also prevented them from holding public office and from entering mainstream professions such as law, pharmacy, teaching, and accounting. Excluded from Canadian society at large, yet determined to create a place for themselves in this country, they established themselves in resource industries. By the 1930s, the issei, the first generation of Japanese Canadians, had built communities around the fishing and lumber industries, in the town of Steveston at the mouth of the Fraser River, and in towns and settlements along the coast and on Vancouver Island. Lucrative berry farms and market gardens had been developed in many areas of the Fraser Valley. In Vancouver, in the district around Powell Street, called "Nihonjin-machi" ("Japanese Town"), they lived, worked and shopped in a bustling urban centre of shops, hotels, restaurants and residential homes.

As the second-generation nisei came of age in the late 1930s, they appeared to be on the verge of reaping the economic benefits of their issei parents' labours. While still denied the vote in BC, as the Canadian-born children of immigrant parents, the nisei were educated to believe in democratic principles and civil liberties, and so were hopeful that the racist barriers which had always been imposed on them would eventually be lifted. At the outset of the next decade, however, their optimism was severely undermined — and their faith in Canadian democracy tested to its very limits. Shortly after the bombing of Pearl Harbor on December 7, 1941, the entire social and economic fabric of this Japanese Canadian community was torn apart by the actions of their government

THE MASS UPROOTING

Just days after the bombing, Japanese-language newspapers were closed down and fishing boats were impounded, putting some 1,800 Japanese Canadian fishermen out of work. These first restrictions were seen by members of the community as needless and unfounded "precautionary measures" taken by a government caught up in the war hysteria of the time. Nevertheless, they believed that no further measures would be taken if they tolerated this over-reaction and reminded the Canadian government that they were, after all, Canadian citizens. They were certainly not prepared for the Liberal government's decisions following swiftly on these first two restrictions.

As citizens loyal to this country, Japanese Canadians assumed that their government would recognize their civil liberties. An editorial of January 4, 1942, in the community's newspaper, the *New Canadian*, dismissed as "silly" the rumours that they might be expelled from BC. Editor Tom Shoyama added, "The idea of camps equivalent to internment camps is also branded in the same light."

The first premonition of disaster came on January 14, when the government passed Order in Council PC 365 which designated an area 100-miles inland from the west coast as a "protected area." All male Japanese nationals aged 18 to 45 were to be removed from this zone and taken to road camps in the Jasper area of BC. Even this order, though considered extreme and unnecessary, was tolerated by most nisei — as "aliens," Japanese male nationals could be expected to accept some restrictions. Moreover, assurances had been given by the government that PC 365 was only a temporary "security measure," and that Canadians of Japanese ancestry need not fear such treatment.

Within three weeks — with a shock that threw the Japanese Canadian community into tumult — Order in Council PC 1486 was passed, expanding the power of the Minister of Justice to remove any and all persons from a designated protected zone. This blanket power was then applied to one group alone — "all persons of Japanese racial origin." This new policy radically altered the status of Japanese Canadians. From February 25, 1942, their Canadian birthright became meaningless, and henceforth they were to be judged solely on the basis of their racial ancestry, not on their citizenship, or even the country of their birth. The War Measures Act legalized the government actions, even though they were based on racist precepts and not necessary by military standards for national security. The stigma of "enemy alien" made Japanese Canadians outcasts in their own country.

On March 4, 1942, the BC Security Commission was established, chaired by Vancouver industrialist Austin Taylor, with RCMP Assistant Commissioner Frederick J. Mead and Assistant Commissioner of the BC Provincial Police, John Shirras. It was this civilian body that was empowered to carry out the systematic expulsion of "all persons of Japanese racial origin" from the area within 100 miles of the BC coast. A "Custodian of Enemy Property" was authorized to administer and hold "in trust" the properties and belongings of these people.

As the uprooting began, a dusk-to-dawn curfew was imposed on all Japanese Canadians. Houses could be entered at all times of the day and night and searched by RCMP officers without a warrant. Cameras and radios were confiscated, cars impounded, and removal notices were handed out.

Thousands of Japanese Canadians, rounded up like cattle, were herded into Vancouver from the coastal towns and Vancouver Island. Many had been given as little as 24 hours to vacate their homes. Chaos, terror and disbelief infected the community as families were split apart and men were hastily shipped off to road camps. In Vancouver, Hastings Park with its Pacific National Exhibition (PNE) buildings, was used as a "clearing site" before people were shipped away from the coast. Conditions in the park were degrading and barbaric, the women and children were segregated and forced to live in the Livestock Buildings. Many of these unfortunate individuals were confined there for months, eating substandard food, without knowing where they would end up or what had become of their husbands, families, and relatives.

CONFISCATION AND SALE OF PROPERTIES

On January 19, 1943, the Canadian government passed Order in Council PC 469 giving the Custodian of Enemy Property the power to sell, without the owners' consent, properties which had initially been held "in trust." This new measure, compounding the injustice of the forced uprooting, led to the dispossession of Japanese Canadians. With the dismantling of their community, their former social and economic presence on the west coast could now be erased.

In the spring and summer of 1943, the properties, businesses, houses, and personal effects of all uprooted Japanese Canadians were liquidated by the Custodian of Enemy Property, and many precious belongings, furniture, pianos, sewing machines, and household goods, were sold or auctioned off at a mere fraction of their value. Trunks full of invaluable family heirlooms, dishes, kimonos, silver, and other objects of personal value — which had been stored away for safekeeping — were auctioned off unopened, many for as low as two dollars a piece. Almost overnight, the intricate social and economic infrastructure of the community was destroyed. Now rootless, dispossessed, and faced with an indefinite period of confinement, Japanese Canadians were no longer able to look forward to returning to their homes on the coast.

The government justified the Custodian's actions as an "efficient" economic policy: the proceeds from the liquidation of the assets of the community would be used to pay for the living expenses of the uprooted Japanese Canadians. Unlike prisoners of war or enemy nationals under the Geneva Convention, Japanese Canadians were forced to pay for their own internment. By this action, the Canadian government had imposed on a group of its own citizens who happened to be of Japanese ancestry, a status lesser than that of nationals from enemy countries.

The politicians and individuals who had been intent on expelling Japanese Canadians from BC, since long before the war, had now finally and successfully used "the politics of racism" to achieve their ends.

An excerpt from Justice In Our Time: The Japanese Canadian Redress Settlement, *Talonbooks and The National Association of Japanese Canadians, 1991.*

LAST STAND

BY RICHARD MANNING

WE WERE VISITING Gold Creek's valley, where Champion now owns and has mostly cut at least one-hundred square miles of land. There is very little checkerboarding in Gold Creek. Instead, it lies under a mostly continuous blanket of Champion's ownership. It feeds the mill at Bonner. As we drove up that drainage, Gallacher and I became more and more excited, because it appeared we were going to find the photos that would document our story well. My Jeep had travelled a full fifteen miles up dusty logging roads, passing through devastated clearcuts the whole way. It was as if we had somehow left what we knew as Montana. The valley that holds Gold Creek is but ten air miles from Missoula, but it is strategically screened from the major highway nearby. There is no reason to drive into the drainage other than to cut trees. We and most Montanans never visit places like this, a sort of loggers' hell.

On previous trips, Gallacher and I had seen mile on mile of hard-cut land, yet nothing like this, a once-forested mountain valley worked as hard as a strip mine. Champion had "slicked off" (the local term for a clearcut, one the loggers themselves use) its land in other areas of the state, but most of its land elsewhere is interspersed with federal, state, and private holdings. In this drainage, the contiguous ownership makes the evidence of the corporation's work roll out to the horizon like a tidal wave of deforestation.

As we drove, the cuts became progressively fresher, meaning we were nearing active logging sites. We could have found logging faster by accepting company tours, but for the obvious reason, we went about this business the hard way. We did not want to see what the corporations wanted us to see, so we searched. That involved driving a few miles then stopping and listening for the whine of chainsaws on the spring air.

After a couple of hours, we heard a saw clatter from a distant ridge and headed toward it. A logger named Kevin Rausch was reworking a seed-tree cut, a common logging technique. On the fist pass, loggers all but clearcut an area, leaving standing only a single mature Western Larch on every half acre or so. That produces a forest covered with trees about as thickly as goalposts cover a football field. After those parent trees have shed a few years' worth of cones to seed the next generation, loggers cut them down, which Rausch was doing. He worked on a ridgetop commanding a view that summed the recent history of Gold Creek. Stretching to the sky behind him were mile on mile of bald slopes webbed by steep gravel roads for logging trucks and fingered by the trails of the cats that had skidded the trees.

Before now, I had seen this spot only on computer. I had crunched through the state tax records which revealed that Champion had cut most of its trees. Yet I had no feel for that statistic until I saw it printed on the land by the mile. Officially, foresters from both Plum Creek and Champion had told me such scenes did not exist, that, yes, they were cutting, but they were using techniques to ensure regrowth of the forests and to prevent erosion. Yet erosion and tactics that cause erosion were everywhere. Topsoil was visible in flight. True, the next generation of trees were being seeded, but how could it grow when the integrity of the soil was so undermined? This was not a question I had to form. This was a question as clearly visible on the land as the rutted skid trails that raised it.

When we spotted Rausch, Gallacher understood immediately that he was looking at an image that told the complete story. He bolted from the Jeep and began loping straight up the hill, hurdling stumps and brush as he went. Gallacher is in his late thirties and still in solid physical shape. He has to be to support his constant frenetic pace. He exists mostly as a ball of energy. Still, the scene before us made him a bit more frantic than usual as he vaulted up the hill like a large ape.

He got the photo he was after: a single frame shows a background of skid trails and clearcuts, with Rausch – suspenders, grimy pants, hard hat, logger boots, and Swedish chain saw – collected in the foreground of the 35-mm frame. A middle-aged larch cut clear through at the stump is falling, frozen by the shutter as it leans to the right and off the frame. The scene shows little but stumps made and stumps in making, and both of us, on seeing it, felt that split of loyalties that eventually plagues most journalists. We had captured the image we knew was bound for Page One. As reporters, we had done our jobs, but as humans, we wished we had never seen that place.

This schism between work and place showed up repeatedly, not just in us, but in those we met on this story. Rausch shared it. In simpler times, he had learned a craft regarded as honorable. Now, though, he works in this new world of the endless clearcuts that make a sustainable partnership with the forest impossible. Rausch does not like his role. I am not guessing about this because I talked to him for a bit, the sort of contact that had intimidated me in the early days of the story. Gallacher and I were photographing the loggers and speaking to them amid scenes of such obvious environmental poundings that we at first figured the loggers would resent us. We were pointing a public and accusing finger at the way they made their living, and no one can like that.

Yet throughout the story, we found the loggers to be frank and approachable, willing to speak, but often resigned to the paradox of their lives. They did not like what they were doing, but it was the work they knew, and the work that at once bound them to and split them from these mountains. Rausch felt the bind as he answered my questions. He glanced grimly over the sweep of clearcuts behind him then said, "Maybe if we would do a better job, the environmentalists would get off our backs."

Rausch was telling us something important: this story was not so much about the cutting of trees as it was about the ways in which we cut trees. These days, our methods are all aimed at profit, or more precisely, profit in the next quarter as opposed to profit twenty years hence. In this taking of the forests for our own benefit, an act as old as humans, there are compromises to be made in the interest of ensuring a future. There are ways to cut that can ease the pain. In Montana, it was not news that industry was cutting trees, but what was news was that quietly, over nearly a decade and out of public view, the industry had responded to tough times by giving no quarter. The industry existed to get wood out and get it whacked into studs, plywood, and cardboard boxes as fast and as cheaply as possible. That was news and a story the bulldozers showed.

We found the dozers that day simply by asking Rausch where they were. They wouldn't be skidding the trees he had cut for a few days, but Rausch said that over there, off toward the horizon, hidden in one of the draws that veined the drainage, we would find the cats. We thanked Rausch, climbed into the Jeep and bounced over more miles of logging roads, over ridges, around the switchbacks until we finally found the cats. They were exactly as my sources told me they would be, working slopes almost too steep to climb on foot. If that same ridge were on public land where rules govern forest practices, those cats would not have been there at all. Those slopes were far too steep for tractor skidding under federal guidelines. Instead, the Forest Service would have required a gentler aerial system of cables to snake logs upslope. Cats churn the topsoil and make it vulnerable to erosion, especially vulnerable here on slopes so precipitous. Yet cats are about half as expensive as any other method of skidding.

Gallacher and I left the Jeep and scrambled over stumps and brush to the top of a protected ridge where we could set up telephoto lenses. Gallacher's motor drives spun through roll after roll. I watched through binoculars. The cats worked. The cats started from a logging road at the toe of the slope and quartered their way toward the top of a clearcut so fresh that most of the shrubs and grasses of a sheltered forest floor were still standing and green. It was a bit like looking at the intact living room of a house after the roof and walls had been removed by a tornado.

At the top of the ridge, the cats pivoted and pointed their blades straight down slope along already-well-grooved trails. Immediately, they dropped their blades for a bite of soil, a method of slowing their descent. Brakes alone would not check the momentum of the behemoths on these steep slopes. As the cats neared piles of felled logs, the operators set the blades down hard to jam them to a full stop, scouring another bite of soil. The operator left the cat and pulled a cable called a choker from a series of such cables wound on a winch that looked like a big yo-yo on the rear of the cat.

The operator set the choker on a log, winched it to the cat, then clomped the choker on to the next log. He repeated the whole process until a half dozen or so logs were tethered to the crawler. Then the cat headed on down the hill, with the blade still biting, tracks pivoting and screeching, with the butts of logs rooting a deep furrow straight down the fall line. Anywhere else, that furrow would be called a ditch, an instant watercourse inviting erosion. Gallacher's cameras churned, recording scene after scene that was not supposed to exist. Over the weeks we had been on the story, we had asked industry people repeatedly about just such practices, and they denied them, said that forestry was about enlightenment and stewardship and respect for the land. Yet we stood on the hillside that day and saw only a torturing of the land, soil sent downhill by the blade of a cat or churned and left naked and helpless before the force of the first rushing thunderstorm.

Gallacher and I spent a couple of hours documenting the destruction, and then we left Gold Creek. I began to understand skid trails and the significance of having this scene multiplied across Montana. Those trails scoured by the cats are repeated every hundred feet or so on almost any steep clearcut. At that rate, a section of land, a square mile, can accommodate more than two hundred such trails, each a quarter mile long. Champion International owns about thirteen hundred sections of land in western Montana. So does Plum Creek, and each plans to have cut all of it by the close of the century. The force of this multiplication can only sink in after you have stood in an old skid trail, as I once did, where rain and cats had eroded it four feet deep, laying bare a cross section, first of detritus, topsoil and organic decay, then of volcanic ash, then of glacial gravels. The wealth of the eons squandered in a few passes of the cat that wrings a few more pennies from an eight-foot two-by-four.

Each of these thousands of skid trails runs down hill, as does water, first to ephemeral streams and freshets, then to creeks, then to rivers like the Big Blackfoot. There what we knew as topsoil becomes silt, and fish die in the translation. Silt gathers in the spaces between rocks where trout deposit eggs, smothering both the eggs and young trout. In a few years, once vibrant trout streams become sterile ditches, broken by the work of carrying topsoil away. This river was the setting of Norman Maclean's *A River Runs Through It*, a story of family, place, and fly fishing. Now trout fishermen bypass the Big Blackfoot because the fish are mostly gone. Biologists suspect sediment from logging is at fault.

In interest not of logging but of cheaper logging methods, we squander our soil, trees, and fish. An honest man – corporate or otherwise – probably would admit this is unwise, and he did, or at least Jim Runyon did. Runyon was the forester and corporate official

Champion designated to speak to me about all of this when I told the company I was investigating its timber practices. I still don't know what to make of that choice, because Runyon was, at least by the standards of other corporate sources I have dealt with in my years as a reporter, unusually forthcoming. Runyon was also a man in a bind, and he talked first about that on a Friday afternoon in May a few weeks after we had visited Gold Creek. Gallacher and I met him at his office in Champion's Montana headquarters, a simple wood building in sight of the Bonner mill. Runyon is a tall, friendly man whose kind eyes are set off by a handlebar mustache and wire-rimmed glasses. In jeans and Oxford-cloth shirt, he settled comfortably into conversation.

Still, he toed the company line, spouted the logic that drives timber corporations, and internally at least, that logic is compelling. There are variations on this theme within the industry, but basically the argument boils to this: to survive in an international economy one must offer the world market competitively priced goods, be they two-by-fours, computers, or hamburgers. Accepting that condition, though, indentures a local industry to the harsh rule of international prices, a particularly onerous burden for Montana's timber industry. Western Montana is a place only barely hospitable to trees. Compared to more sodden regions such as the Pacific Northwest, our trees grow slowly, sparsely, out of the way at the end of long, steep, and expensive gravel roads. Our timber-producing lands are on the economic margins, which shows up in higher costs of production for our wood products. If the area is to hold its own in international markets, then it must find ways to shave costs. To a large degree, the industry does this by mining logs in the cheapest way it can.

If the great invisible hand of the market were as rational and unifying as some article of economic faith would hold, it seems a practical solution to the problem in our forests would emerge. That is, society simply would not produce lumber from marginal lands, but would satisfy demand from more productive places. In a free-market utopia, the marginal lands would be priced out of the game, at least until a shortage pushed the price to the point that loggers might operate on marginal lands both responsibly and profitably.

Unfortunately, this is not a unified system. Champion and Plum Creek, with their considerable investment in Montana, are not about to bow out in deference to Weyerhaeuser or Boise Cascade and those latter companies' more productive land further west. Champion and Plum Creek's executives will tighten the screws, scrimp, save, and cut corners to stay in the game. They must compensate for the handicap dealt by the rocky, steep, and dry land. It is what the corporate system expects from them. They will say what industry has always said: they do this to avoid closing mills, to save thousands of jobs and prevent the collapse of the local economy. They may not be doing it for precisely that reason but it doesn't matter, because if the mills did close, that economic upheaval surely would happen. There is pain in this, because guys like Runyon are right: guys like Rausch have a choice between a disagreeable job and no job at all.

What does this invisible hand of the international market care for our trees, or for men like Runyon and Rausch for that matter, and who should know that better than they do? In Runyon I encountered resignation. The preconceptions that took me into this story and what I saw happening on corporate lands led me to expect predatory archetypes of capitalist mythology overseeing all of this. To a degree I did find such people. Just as often, though, I found people who behaved like prey, who saw themselves on a lower niche in the food chain of laissez faire capitalism.

Runyon weighed in on the latter side early in our interviews when he acknowledged without equivocation (unlike Plum Creek's Bill Parson) that, yes, Champion had decided for strictly competitive reasons to cut all of its own lands in the matter of a decade or so, far faster than those trees could grow back. He said the strategy was based on a cold calculation that once its trees were gone, Champion could use its economic and political clout to pry loose a supply of logs from public, especially Forest Service, lands. The reason was simple: Champion did not have to pay for logs from its own lands, so could use that economic advantage to survive depressed prices for wood products that emerged in the early eighties.

"It was one of those situations where somebody had to make a decision," Runyon said. "We may not want to do it, but if we want to be here and survive tomorrow, we may have to."

Other sources within Champion said that the early part of the decade also brought a fundamental shift in attitudes within the corporation. That is, foresters who once were encouraged to think long term, to consider the next generation of trees, were told vociferously (in one case, in literally a table-pounding session) that "long-term" was defined as next year. It was the shift in philosophy that sicced the cats on the hills.

That table-pounding punctuated a shift that went down hard for foresters, who are by inclination and training more geared to growing trees than cultivating P&L statements. In our first interview, that conflict rang in Runyon, both a forester and executive. I had brought the slides that Gallacher had shot of the cats. After about a half hour of relatively innocuous questions, I dropped the photographs on his desk. He looked at them for a long time then joked with me: "Tell me these were shot on Plum Creek's land."

Then he stared at one shot of a cat's blade gouging the slope and he began talking like a forester, assessing with an expert's eye the performance of the cats:

> *If he [the cat operator] is dropping his blade, then the impact is going to be a whole hell of a lot greater. There's no question about that. It looks like he's basically creating just a huge erosion path through there....He's taking the soil and it's going to end up down in Gold Creek. You're right. I don't make any bones about that. And as a forester that ticks me off, because as a forester I was taught a long time ago that everybody says I am managing a stand of timber, but that's not the true resource. The resource is what the trees are growing in and that's the soil....If he just rips the hell out of the topsoil, then I have lost a fair portion of my acreage [but] to say that does not occur would be lying....I'm not going to lie. It happens.*

Here is a statement that cuts straight across the grain of the public myth that shelters the industry. We suffer the cutting of trees here only to the extent that the industry is able to grow new trees. The industry spares no expense in public-relations gimmickry designed to convince us of this, even to convince us that they grow trees better once they have replaced nature's ill-designed forests with tree factories of their own devising.

BE ALL YOU CAN BE — TAKE ORDERS AND DON'T THINK

BY PAUL RICHARDS

"As a soldier in the Army Reserve, you'll earn a good, steady extra income, learn a valuable career skill and have some exciting opportunities to travel."

ARMY PAMPHLET U.S. GPO 1988 - 542-033/80001

"There's a camaraderie. A closeness that comes from sharing new experiences with new friends in a country far different from your own."

ARMY PAMPHLET U.S. GPO 1988 - 506810

"The president also said he signed an order extending the Pentagon's call-up of reservists for up to two years. The order was intended to keep on duty reservists beyond the 180-day maximum previously authorized.

And the order allows Bush to summon up to 1 million reservists, although the administration says it does not envision a call-up that large."

THE ASSOCIATED PRESS, JAN. 18, 1991

71

LAST JANUARY, the U.S. Army recruited me. They needed someone to help them bend the news. The Army had bucks. I, having recently left Associated Press, had none. Could we work something out?

No, I wasn't ready to leave Montana.

Okay, said the recruiter, how about a deal with the Army Reserves? Good pay, minimal time investment, and you get to stay home.

Here's the skinny: You'll pull down 900 bucks a month, plus room and board for 18 weeks training (8 weeks basic, 10 weeks Army journalism at Fort Jackson, S.C.). Then, you'll get $120 a weekend, only one-month required.

If you "play your cards right," in "no time at all" you'll be a second lieutenant at $1500 a month full-time, $220 a weekend.

Throw in a $1500-to-$3000 enlistment bonus, up to $33,600 in education bonuses, PX and commissary privileges, free medical and dental benefits, life insurance, retirement benefits, flights to Europe for $13, and flights anywhere in the United States, including Hawaii and Puerto Rico, for $10.

Tempting bait? You bet! Not every magazine or newspaper offers perks like that.

Lieutenant Richards

From a freelance writer — broke, working twice as hard as normal people for half the money, no health insurance, no dental plan, no subsidized groceries, no discounted tape decks or other PX goodies — to the good life with but one easy stroke of the pen.

All I would have to do is justify invading foreign countries and killing people.

"You could be down there in Panama right now, working the news media," said Sgt. "We-don't-go-by-first-names" Owen during one of our get-togethers at a local bowling alley. As I mused upon this, a young skinhead with muscles bulging recognized Owen and sauntered towards table. "When you gonna sign me up?" he asked loudly, "I wanna go kick Nicaraguan ass."

After the muscular one left, I asked Sgt. Owen what would happen if I didn't actually support invading Panama, Grenada, Nicaragua, Guatemala, Vietnam, the Philippines, Lebanon, or whatever small country chosen by some insecure President?

Startled, Sgt. Owen didn't answer.

Was there any way Lt. Richards could refuse orders to sugarcoat war-mongering and *not* end up in time in the stockade for insubordination?

Sgt. Owen drew a blank.

If I honored my own principles and ended up in jail, wouldn't that expose the Army's slogan, "Be All You Can Be," as cruelly cynical? Taking orders and not thinking for myself — is *that* all I can be?

After a few uncomfortable moments, Owen put my enlistment papers back into his briefcase, unsigned, and we pleasantly said goodbye. I never heard from him again.

Body Bag Quotas

Now, I read where Sgt. Owen and his fellow recruiters can't meet quotas. It seems many others share my qualms about invasion by whim (despite retread Vietnam-era presidential assurances that full-scale overseas assaults are merely defensive in nature). Even the good-pay-and-you-get-to-stay-home Army Reserve has lost its appeal.

I recently watched a hundred area Army reservists muster for Saudi Arabian duty. Leaving the warm Armory in downtown Bozeman at day's end, they hunched themselves against darkness and bitter cold. But, something made them stop and suddenly straighten.

Through steam from their own respiration, the reservists looked across the street at over 300 people holding candles, quietly standing in below-zero weather, a poignant vigil for peace.

The reservists were stunned. But, there was no hatred or disdain, no obvious cynicism or ridicule, directed at protestors, or at reservists. The unflappable allegiance to my-country-right-or-wrong that generated so much foreign and domestic violence 20 years ago had matured with the wisdom brought home by survivors of Vietnam.

Let's Party!

That night, reservists gathered at a local motel with family and friends for a very stoic "party." On the surface, everything was fine. Freshly-shorn males and heavily-made-up females engaged in subdued conversations, nervous laughter and superficial bravado.

These were simple confused folk, just the type that body bags are made for. They just wanted extra income for tuition or the kids' Christmas presents. They never thought George Bush was mad enough to risk their lives for big oil companies, mid-Eastern feudalism, and the United States' right to waste. They never dreamed of commemorating this birthday of the Prince of Peace by going to war.

"He (Bush) went all around the globe to line up support for the invasion," said one reservist friend, "but he never came to his own country, he never asked us for permission."

Almost painfully, the troops went through the motions of their "party." True emotions were repressed with military aplomb. Outwardly, tears did not flow, but this observer noted countless red eyes.

The whole evening was out of step. Kegs donated by patriotic local beer distributors were hardly touched.

A happy-faced blow-dried deejay from K-B-O-Z Radio clapped his hands to get attention and proclaimed: "Hey everybody, there's music in the next room! Plenty of beer left! Let's dance!"

The deejay then tried to lead a procession to the dance floor. Excepting one reporter, no one followed. The deejay started the music anyway. It was a John Lennon tune.

Monster Trucks

Back at a friend's hotel room, I watched a TV commercial plugging the appearance of "Monster Trucks — Live" at a nearby city. With deep intonation usually reserved for second-rate rock concerts or wrestling matches, a ballsy announcer described how the enormous trucks mangle other vehicles and brave walls of flame.

But his deepest ballsiest voice commanded reverence for "The World's Largest Transformer," an upright mechanical contraption that crushes cars and trucks in crab-like claws.

Witness evil on parade: Senseless consumption and rampant materialism capped by sacrificial demolition. Cultural psychosis, routine commercial television fare, now extended — live — to the discerning public for only ten bucks.

The commercial gave new perspective to Sgt. Owen and the nondancing reservists:

> *Our society is out of kilter. The mindless destruction of "Monster Trucks" is the same gleeful maladjustment that prompts mechanics to mash cars in demolition derbies every summer, the same unspoken anger that causes farmers in north central Montana to crunch into each other's combines at county fairs, the same candy-*

coated malady that draws thousands to automobile races in hopes of
fatal crashes, and the same unacknowledged sickness that causes a
former oil company executive and Central Intelligence Agency
director to promote war.

Our way of life is at stake, he tells us, so we must kill.

Our way of life is at stake, with its diseased greed, fatal addiction to fossil fuels, and refusal to accept change and personal responsibility.

Our way of life is at stake. How could we live without "monster Trucks" crushing all before them, "The World's Largest Transformer" snipping cars in half, and similar obscene rituals of destruction.

Our way of life is at stake. We are the conquerors of the world — how can renewable energy sources, sustainable economics, stable communities, and other peace dividends compare with that?

Our way of life is at stake, so we tender the lives of these 100 Army reservists.

War Always Comes Home

Can we pause here to look at the last moment of another 100 young Americans who defended "our way of life"?

Last year, as I slept at the Tibetan Cultural Center in Missoula — after honoring the Feb. 26 Tibetan New Year and mourning the Chinese occupation — someone across the alley yelled "Freeze!"

I woke with a start to hear a response: no words, just a visceral roar of distilled anger, defiance, and anguish. Then, as the growl tapered off, the pop-pop-pop of firearms.

By the time I got there, the guy face down in the street was warm, but most certainly dead from the police fusillade. In early morning darkness, his blood pooled black.

Before he bought it, he drank coffee quietly for three hours in a nearby all-night restaurant, then pulled out his .44 Magnum and calmly blew away another customer sitting at the counter and a hapless restaurant janitor.

The janitor was dead, the patron dying.

Turned out the customer lived, thanks to exceptional care from police and medical personnel. Also turned out the fellow with his face in the street, Clifford Harper, had been the sole remaining survivor of a group of 100 Marines ferried into North Vietnam by helicopter. Within two weeks, 94 died in battle.

Of the six who returned home, five committed suicide during the ensuing 20 years. Harper was the last of the 100.

"He said he felt dirty inside, filthy dirty inside," said Harper's father, Jim. "I was always afraid something like this would happen."

Harper's stepmother, Susie, said, "He'd get to talking about this (Vietnam) stuff, and he'd get tears in his eyes. Don't make him out to be a murderer."

STRADDLING THE VOLCANOES

INTERVIEW WITH OMAR CASTAÑEDA
BY TERRI LEE GRELL

Omar Castañeda was born surrounded by active volcanoes in his native land of Guatemala. His writing tends toward magic realism with themes that include cultural conflict, the twin drives toward assimilation and confrontation, and the reformation of belief under drastic social change. All explosive issues. But he is far from an explosive character himself, though his sense of humor erupts quickly, and usually with a sting. It seemed appropriate to talk about his work, including his recent young adult novel, Among the Volcanoes, *under the shadow of Mount St. Helens in Longview, Washington. Omar read selections from his new novel and from* Cunuman *(a 1987 adult novel about social change in Guatemala) at Lower Columbia College last Spring. During his visit, Terri Lee Grell, journalist and editor of* Lynx *magazine, talked with Omar about magic realism, feminism, political activism and his popular courses on shamanism and "Literature of the Unreal" at Western Washington University, where he has taught for the last three years.*

Omar has earned several awards for creative writing and folklore, including a Fulbright Senior Research Grant to his native Guatemala where he spent part of last summer researching the sequel to Among the Volcanoes. *Extensive readings of Mayan-mythology, particularly the* Popol Vuh, *the sacred text of the Quiché Maya, inspire his works, but it is the authenticity of his writing the woman's voice — women as mothers, daughters and wives — that sets Omar apart from his contemporaries. The women are "emblems of Guatemala," Omar says, because they are caught in the conflicts between tradition and acceptance of foreign views.*

TERRI LEE GRELL: Cunuman....*that's an interesting name...*

OMAR CASTAÑEDA: One time, a reviewer spelled it "Cuntman."

I can see it now, is it a bird, a plane? No, it's Cuntman! We're saved!

I have characters called Xtah and Xpuch. One reviewer called them Ish-push and Ish-shove...that's hilarious...but "Cuntman"?

Maybe it's a fraudulent — oops, I mean Freudian — slip. Which leads me to ask why the heroes in your novels are always women.

I'm very concerned with women's issues. My politics are founded on a lot of other issues too — problems of racism, Central American politics, classism. But I finally see gender issues as the most fundamental. I see a complex structure of power struggles. I locate the origin of certain needs and requirements of individuals to gain power and to diminish others as a way of survival. I locate that in sexual politics.

I don't agree with the so-called "radical" premise that promotes feminism as the be-all, end-all.

I know a lot of feminists who I don't agree with in their politics, and who I think are arguing lines that are probably not very healthy for themselves and other people. But there's a certain kind of value in arguing at any time in a political movement. There are different levels of aggressiveness, of straight-line views. And these are important because at the same time, at any given moment in a movement, there are also a great variety of audiences to hear those views. One person can affect people on the same level of attitude, whereas the others may not be affected. When there's a lag time in the political movement, you always need front-line, adamant people, aggressive people to break down the really difficult barriers, the first barricades in a very hostile countryside. There are other people who are perhaps more detached, less angry, less vehement, who have a wider perspective on the movement itself. It is unfortunate that less-angry people will sometimes sacrifice those very adamant front-line people. The general motion in a political picture may go to a point where people say, "These vehement people are no longer helpful to the group." Maybe feminism has advanced to the point where there are people who are still so anti-male, who were extremely important at a time — and may still be extremely important in certain places — but have been seduced by power or are too straight-line in their thinking, and the movement as a whole may not be so well-served by them anymore.

Tell me more about the women in your novels, what they stand for, and their relationship to your research into the Popol Vuh.

My main characters are women who are discovering themselves. They are emblems of Guatemala, one way or another. They have allegiance to some of the traditions they have been raised with and they realize that those same traditions are hurting them, damaging them, and they try to invent some new possibilities for themselves. They fight against the easy acceptance of foreign views. So the symbolism becomes quite easy to make. In the *Popol Vuh* there's a Creator Mother that figures prominently — Xmucane. She goes by various names. Sometimes it's Great Grandmother, or Grandmother, or Mother or Woman with Children. Sometimes it's Cacao Woman. But there's a constant pairing going on so that even in a given instant you have the guise of a female force, a female-like manifestation that's just one guise of a pair that also has its male counterpart. But it happens that the female side in it has greater play. She figures prominently. In my novel *Among the Volcanoes*, the woman is fighting against the gender roles of her culture and trying to invent something new for herself, while battling with specific American interests. This becomes the emblem for the larger issues of Guatemala trying to do that. It also becomes an issue of what I'm trying to do as a writer, in my own biculturality. I also see this as one of the main threads of the *Popol Vuh*. There is very much an awareness of the clash of cultures. There is both sustaining the continuity of the tradition and the unavoidable fact that one must invent self anew, and that the foreign influence coming in is not necessarily a good one. The foreign influence brings something of value, but it's overall not particularly good.

Sounds like the tragedy of the "discovery of America."

79

There you go. It's not the discovery of America, it's the *conquest* of America. The reality in Guatemala is not 500 years celebration of the discovery, it's 500 years of *resistance*. In October, 1990, we had a Dia de la Raza celebration. It was an anti-quincentennial celebration.

Western Washington will have similar things, culminating in October, 1992. For that time I've devised a course called "Literature of the Maya" which will look at the *Popol Vuh* and other literature just after the conquest. We'll discuss that right at the conquest time. I think the Western states will have lots of activity connected with that. Last year, there was a Pan-Native American gathering in Quito, Ecuador. The next will take place in Guatemala. All of this is a gearing up for Pan-Native American unity. That's the focal point.

How do you unify themes of Maya myth and history in your work?

I use a structure and certain motifs that I see in the *Popol Vuh* to inform the structure and motifs in *Cunuman*. The *Popol Vuh* is a kind of myth history. It starts with the origin of the universe and ends with the Spanish conquest of the Maya in Guatemala. But there's no clear line between what we in the West think of as "myth" and "history" or "legend." There's a clear blending, no clear demarcation. This implicates Guatemala to a large extent. A writer is like a neo-mythologizer, I think. Good fiction writing is making up lies or myths that are so believable, there is a curious blend of myth and truth, myth and legend.

Should we say "myths" and "lies" in the same breath?

We can think of myth in terms of the colloquial usage which does mean lie or falsehood. But we can also think of myth in terms of what folklorists call it — sacred belief. In fact, part of what makes a myth sacred is that it deliberately frustrates rational thought. If we go to any myth system — the *Popol Vuh* or the Christian Genesis — and label them as myths the way folklorists do, we see a curious thing. They share a lot of characteristics. They are ahistorical, atemporal, and they usually involve deities or semideities. But they all also deliberately frustrate rational thought. That may be why the West has a more vulgar kind of thinking about myths as lies. We in the West want to have a more rational view. The myth seems beyond belief, like a lie. But a lot of work has been done to use the *Popol Vuh* to understand older traditions. It dates from circa 1550. Dennis Tedlock, cultural anthropologist, places it right around 1558. That's pretty much at the end of the Quiché Maya reign. It talks about historical events that happened up to 400 years before that. But for us, that's prehistory. So these texts are sometimes the only way to understand history that is lost.

That was then, and this is now...

I think America for a long time has had either a cavalier attitude towards the lack of humanitarian practices in Guatemala or has actively condoned very malicious practices down there. Guatemala is a very unfortunate place. Amnesty International has listed many years of political horror stories there. People disappear all the time, people get killed all the time. Investigations just don't happen. Virtually every family in Guatemala has members of its family murdered, found brutally murdered...

But we only hear about drug trafficking between governments. Then our government justifies its threats to intervene.

Yes, exactly. Recently Guatemala was put on the list of places that were either growing certain narcotics or were part of the traffic. So there has been heavy use of defoliants on crops. But the defoliants, coincidentally, have been used in areas that were cited as spots of guerilla activity, insurgency areas. You only hear about drug trafficking because it is all a pretext. What they're really after is keeping down the insurgency. The U.S. has helped the Guatemalan government — that is, the Guatemalan military — by training them for anti-insurgency. This is a general anti-communist attitude that the U.S. government pushes in Central America. It sees Guatemala as one of the last "Domino Pizzas" (laughs) before the horrors of Communism sweep up into the U.S., which is ludicrous. Guatemala has a very strong middle class compared to some of the other Central American countries. It also has a history of very strong military government, so it has a lot of control on the people. In the olden days there used to be a lot of big business in Guatemala, foreign business. You still find that. Going way back, you find the United Fruit Company. More recently, large plantation owners and people who claim they are doing "forestry," but what they do is take out a lot of wooded areas by cutting down the Peten (rain forest area) for pasture lands for big cattle industries. Most of the land is in fact owned by foreign companies.

So your writing has reflected some of your objective political concerns, which is ironic, since you're tagged as a fabulist, a magic realist.

In the U.S. people tend to think of Gabriel García-Márquez as one of the originators of magic realism. He's very political. In fact, there's not many Latin American writers who are not political. It seems like we think that only in *this* country can writers somehow be artists and

81

not political. In fact, the mindset here is that you *ought* to separate the two. Most of the world — but let me just speak about Latin America… Hispanics think that is simply preposterous. Someone who can make that separation is in fact making a political statement. They are taking the stance that they are absolute collaborators with the status quo. That *is* their political statement. To make no statement is to say, "everything is fine." But in countries where there is torture going on all the time, where people are disappearing, where there are murders that are not investigated, where there are civil rights violations constantly: to say, "everything is fine" is a rather strong statement. So to be a writer is to be political. To use language to inform and illuminate atrocities, that's just part of being a writer.

Is writing a form of self-abuse? I think of shamans…

Yes! And salvation. It's funny…I thought of shamans, too. I used to teach a course called "Shamanism and Literature" which looked at how the writer — particularly the poet — in literate culture has supplanted the shaman in non-literate culture. If you look at the traditional traits in shamanism — things like transformation, vertical travel, self-curing, psychopompos, ecstasy, incantations — and list all these kinds of traits, and then do surveys of poetry, you pinpoint in a random impressionistic way higher percentages of shamanism encoded within good poetry. I always thought that the writer herself is someone who is psychically damaged in some way, and turns to writing as a way to re-harmonize the spirit. In that journey, there is the appeal of the "Great Shaman" which is the tradition of "other" poets, hearing "other" voices. Using writing as a way to reclaim self, to *make* self, and in that she has harmonized herself so well that others can read this thing, this poem, this piece of fiction, and harmonize themselves, too. So there is a shaman in the writer, I believe that.

But the shaman was respected, revered by all. Not so, with contemporary writers, poets now…it's getting more exclusive, the tendency to listen to that damaged part of yourself and give it dignity is —

— an initiation. But remember, too, that when you look at shamans — think of the most famous shamans, Black Elk, Maria Sabina, people like that — when they went into initiation, they were often children, they were either psychically or physically damaged. They were tagged as possibly strong shamans, some because they had epilepsy. Then they went through an initiation ritual, during which they somehow get attached to a great shaman figure. Initiation also involves mutilation and rebirth, a transformation with the help of a "familiar."

The muse.

Yes. And sometimes it is an animal that is speaking and teaching. More than simply "helping." And then there's vertical travel, going up a tree. Ascending and descending to various places. With fishing cultures there's usually a voyage into waters of some type. But there's often going up to the sky in various ways, not horizontal travel. Vertical travel is critical to the initiation. When we think of the shaman we must also think of psychic damage. If we think of them as just epileptic, it's not quite right, because it's not just about physical damage.

Poets and writers in the U.S. don't get that much respect, or empathy, for the damage, the initiation. Is it different in Guatemala?

Yes, because poets and writers there are very involved people. The separation between politics and poetry and art does not exist there. It's not uncommon for them to be intimately involved in government. They become ambassadors, diplomats. The Sandinista government was full of poets. There is a kind of over-sanctioning and appreciation for the writers. It is less so here, in the U.S. We also have a lot of crass commercial writers that dominate the scene. But I think it's still true in the U.S. that when you say by introduction, "This is a writer" or "This is the author of this book," people tend to think, "Oh! A REAL author!" There's still a kind of admiration...

I've done that. "This is so-and-so, the writer!" And everybody at the table has that look on their faces that says, "Who the hell is so-and-so?"

Or worse, "Who cares?" (laughs) Like, "Hey, this is Stephen King!" and they go, "Wasn't he the one in that American Express commercial?!"

83

IF POETS WERE MADE

BY LOWELL JAEGER

I GRADUATED from the Iowa Writers' Workshop, though just barely. The faculty refused to sign my thesis. I was angry with the workshop because I wasn't producing much or growing as a writer. I didn't strain a muscle to help myself either, because my failure was tolerable so long as I could blame my teachers, the university, or the "literary establishment," rather than pointing the finger where it belonged. Back then I was full of all the standard paranoia toward workshops that one still hears on the pages of this or that journal over and over again. Chicken Little sounds the alarm; workshops are cloning McPoets and McPoems, and like a final curtain falling on the literature of Western Civilization, the sky is dropping down, down, down.

Cock-a-doodle-do. I'd enlisted in the Iowa Writers' Workshop to be made into a writer, and because I wasn't performing like I'd hoped, I strutted around the classroom making noise, pecking at my teachers for not doing their jobs. Jack Legget, the workshop director back then, wisely counseled me not to make a lifelong practice of such cocky nonsense, then he overrode the faculty's censure, winked, shook my drumstick, and sent me out into the world where he knew I was doomed to someday contend with students just like myself. "If the fool persists in his folly, he shall become wise." Thus spake William Blake.

Ironically, a reviewer for *American Book Review* panned my first book, *War On War*, for the "glib vacuity" and "sanitized execution" one would expect of a writer who had been groomed by the Iowa Workshop: "A reasonable subtitle for the collection might be 'The

Iowa Writers' Workshop Meets Vietnam,'" said the review; "Jaeger is a former student of this outfit, and his teachers, *the usual suspects*, wax predictably effusive about the prize-hopeful importance of the book." (The italics are mine.) Marvin Bell had written a cover blurb, but he was on leave or teaching in Hawaii for the entire span of my enrollment at Iowa. Denise Levertov penned a strong endorsement also; I'd never spoken to her in my life. Nor had I ever been a student of William Stafford's, and he also wrote a few kind words about the book. In his self-righteous struggle against glib vacuity, the Chicken Little who wrote this review was both glib and vacuous. I'd bet this man worries about being pursued by the "poetry mafia," an old label thrown at successful writers by unhappy wanna-be's.

And Jack Legget was right: I've been teaching now for ten years; every quarter one student or another of mine mirrors for me my behavior at Iowa. I get blamed if my students fail ("But I did it just like *you* said I should!"), and if my students succeed, then I'm blamed for having engineered their careers. One of my students published poems in a magazine that's been rejecting me for years. I overheard a classmate's jealous analysis: "He only got published because he sucks up to Jaeger, and Jaeger's got pull." Strange I can be seen as so powerful when most days I worry that if my salary were determined by how much my students gain from me, then I shouldn't be paid at all.

All this racket in the barnyard begins with the sophomoric notion that a writer can be made — can be guaranteed success — if only he or she enrolls in a prestigious school and makes solid contacts with influential bigshots. "I can get you a gonnection," offers Myer Wolfsheim, and Nick must be comforted to know that Gatsby's not a self-made man. That's how I felt at Iowa; I was convinced that all my classmates who were writing well, placing poems, and winning awards — those guys were all sucking up to the faculty and making "gonnections." So, too, the reviewer mentioned above is comforted to assume I'm a mafioso.

If they're secure enough, some writers share names of editors, prospective markets, etc. Maybe one student in a thousand is recommended by a big-name teacher to an agency. But I know of no writer ever who edged his or her way into the spotlight without having some pretty damn good work to show. Hemingway said the one tool every writer needs is a built-in shockproof crap detector. The notion that workshops can destroy genuine talent, or that workshops can mold the mediocre into literary marketability is crap. A writer weak enough to be broken by a workshop will likely be broken elsewhere anyway. Writers who think they are spending tuition dollars on instant literary success are fated to meet with some painful surprises. And critics who think workshops both ruin writers and then propel them into fame…well, they're just plain naive.

On the other hand, if I've been made at all, I must credit my eighth-grade English teacher, Bernadine Tomasik. At fourteen, I was so strung-out on new hormones I spent most of the year exiled into whatever corner the teachers shoved my desk and thereby drew a DMZ between me and the rest of civilization. (Once the vice-principal jerked me from class and dragged me down the hallway with my head in a hammer lock.) I have no idea what the hell Miss Tomasik was trying to teach me. I had Beatle-mania on the brain; I was scribbling goofy parodies of "I Want to Hold Your Hand" and "Twist and Shout" until Miss Tomasik ventured into my corner and was suddenly looming over my desk, reading my pen scratches. I expected the worst. At that moment she could have wounded me almost as much as I deserved. "Well," she said, "a budding poet. These aren't bad." Somewhere she fanned in me the ember that would someday light my life.

Or my senior year, 1969 — the height of the Vietnam "conflict," — I was scared, depressed, and soon to be of draft-age. I remember sitting in calculus class sunk into such a funk I couldn't lift my pencil or focus on the test at hand. I hadn't been listening all term; body counts on the network news each night were all the numbers I could handle. Mr. Komro confiscated my test sheet, and I heard him wad it and pitch it in the waste basket near his desk in the back of the room. Soon he was headed my way again. I half expected he was going to hit me, but I can't explain why. I hardly knew the man though I'd seem him daily for the past three school years, and I assumed he neither knew anything about me nor cared to know more. He laid a copy of *Harper's* in front of me. "Read this," he said, putting his hand on my shoulder. "I can't understand it, but maybe you can." In front of me were poems and letters of e.e. cummings. I'd never seen a copy of *Harper's* before in my life; I barely knew the name e.e. cummings it was the first time I'd ever read "I Sing of Olaf…." All that weird typography seemed at a glance like formulas in our text, but by God I understood them. Even though I hadn't done my homework.

Miss Tomasik and Mr. Komro lifted me up when they could easily have crushed me, and in that sense they were two of the most valuable connections I've ever made. Shortly after *War On War* hit the bookstores, I found a letter in my box from Bernadine Tomasik. She'd read my work, and she said simply, "I'm proud of you." I hadn't heard from her for better than twenty years. Some will call it corny, but that letter meant more to me — went a lot further toward "making" this poet — than any workshop, cover blurb, or review.

THE LARIATI VERSUS/VERSES THE LITERATI

LOPING TOWARD DANA GIOIA'S DREAM COME REAL

BY PAUL ZARZYSKI

I GREW UP IN a bookless house — except for a bible stored in its original box high out of reach on a closet shelf, and a copy of *Vein of Iron,* the history of the Pick & Mathers iron ore mining company for whom my father worked. My mother, of course, recited a few nursery rhymes to me when I was young. After kindergarten, however, I have little recollection of the nuns at St. Mary's grade school teaching poetry, aside from Sister Mary Ivan ("The Terrible") sentencing us to memorize and recite in front of the class "Paul Revere's Ride" — two lines per violation as punishment. Daniel Bensoni, God bless him wherever he is, sinned his way to a record 80 lines. In much the same way as I went from holy parochial school to hoodlum Hurley High, I fell in one swoop from Mother Goose to poetry-as-penance (say three Our Fathers, three Hail Marys, 30 lines of "Paul Revere's Ride" and go my child and sin no more) to serious study of The Masters in high school literature classes.

In those days, in that isolated neck of the Midwest north woods, Poetry In The Schools programs did not exist. It was easy to make the standard "all-poets-are-dead" deduction. More significantly, however, I decided that none of the poems that we were forced to decode and decipher were about my life, my interests, my passions. Instead of Grecian urns in our house, we had Red Wing crocks, coal buckets, washtubs, and bushel baskets. Moreover, why were there no poems about hunting ducks, fishing for native brookies, making hard hits on the gridiron, running wild between beer joints on a fast motorcycle? If my life didn't matter to the art of poetry, then why should poetry matter to me? At 16, in the midst of a blue-collar environment, this decision to scratch poetry off my Christmas list forever was that simple.

The influences of the subsequent five years, which transformed poetry from foe to partner-for-life, are too involved to delineate now, but I will pinpoint the single poem most responsible for the complete turn-about: "Zimmer, Drunk and Alone, Dreaming of Old Football Games," by renowned poet and editor, Paul Zimmer. I remember asking my freshman composition instructor, David Steingass (my first living poet!), if this was in fact a legitimate poem. Not only was Zimmer writing in concrete images made from a clear, crisp language that dazzled the eye and ear on that first jump out of the chute, he was also addressing experiences and emotions that I could relate to. Poetry, like a friendly ghost, like lightning you could hug without harm, had struck close to home, and I instantly loved the notion that my tiny life might be worthy of such power in song and sentiment. Poetry, all of a sudden, made sense and mattered.

SINCE THE MAY [1991] issue of The Atlantic ran Dana Gioia's essay, "Can Poetry Matter?" I've received six Xeroxes by mail from both writer and non-writer friends, most of whom praised Gioia's comments/accusations. "CAN Poetry Matter?" The title lures both writers and readers of poetry (Gioia maintains that they, unfortunately, are one and the same) to this provocative essay, and, in fact, if you haven't already received your copy, chances are that you soon will — I copied copies of copies and sent them to friends who wrote back and said they followed suit. Little could Dana Gioia have known that he was inventing The Chain Essay. And speaking of "suit," are we all in violation of copyright laws? If so, my apologies to The Atlantic. And to their lawyers, this: my most valuable assets are a 19 year-old buckskin gelding with heaves and a 1971 Chevy Monte Carlo with a flat camshaft (140,000 miles, so far) and running on six and one-half of its eight cylinders — I "make my living" writing and reciting poetry.

I agree, on the whole, with Dana Gioia's thesis that "...although there is a great deal of poetry around, none of it matters very much to readers, publishers, or advertisers — to anyone, that is, except other poets; ...today most readings (mixing so seldom with music, dance, or theatre) are celebrations less of poetry than of the author's ego; ...outside the classroom — where society demands that the two groups interact — poets and the common reader are no longer on speaking terms."

There are, however, exceptions, and cowboy poetry is one of them. That's right, I said "cowboy poetry" as in range rhymes and bunkhouse ballads written and recited by buckaroo bards and cowpuncher poets. Go ahead, chuckle. Better yet, laugh loudly. Cowboy poets welcome laughter, which, in the lives of "regular folks," goes hand in hand with fun. I said chuckle, not snicker. But if the latter comes more naturally to you Literati elitists, first reconsider my thesis: in the Lariati arena, at least three of Gioia's six proposals take root and thrive naturally out of the tradition.

First, cowboy poets "recite other people's works," especially the poems of those who rode/wrote before them. They do so in large part to pay tribute to their legacy and history, and they do so alongside contemporary works to illustrate the continuations and connections in form and focus, as well as the changes, which they deem necessary for the growth of their art. Call it "folk art," if it will make you snicker or squirm any less, but then consider the Texas cowboy poet, Joel Nelson, who often recites Robert Frost's "The Road Not Taken," which, he deems, is about a lot of cowboys he's ridden with over the years. And consider also Rod McQuery from Ruby Valley, Nevada, or Wyoming cowboy poet, Bill Jones, both Viet Nam vets, who've written and recited strong free verse poems about the war we all suffered through. Good poetry is good poetry — whoever, wherever, etc. — and usually reaches toward the universal. Period.

Cowboy poets also fulfill the second Gioia proposal by "mixing poetry with the other arts, especially music, and by planning evenings honoring dead or foreign writers." Thousands of people — mostly non-poets! — pay up to $12 per ticket (sold out months in advance) to these performances, called "Gatherings," in Elko, Nevada at the end of January, in the bitter middle of winter, each year. This western renaissance began in 1985 with the first Cowboy Poetry Gathering, and since then the number of similar celebrations across the U.S. continues to grow. This past April, I recited cowboy poems in D.C. (it's your guess: District of Columbia or Dodge City?) as part of a show called "Poets, Politicians, & Other Storytellers," sponsored by The National Council for the Traditional Arts and The George Washington University. Back-to-back with a lengthy traditional ballad written in the 1880s, I recited my own rhymed and metered poems right alongside the free verse work. As a grand finale to the show, the Legendary Ray Hicks told his engaging Jack Tales. Like most cowboy poetry gatherings combining musicians, storytellers, a cappella soloists, and theatrical presentations, the latter which often include verse, the DC performance offered a variety of forms. The response was enthusiastic, once again proving that audiences of wide variation in sentiment, lifestyle, whatever, have turned out on both coasts to, as my mentor and friend Dick Hugo so often put it, "have fun with the sounds of words."

In the fifth entry of his "wishlist sextet," Gioia states that "The sheer joy of the art must be emphasized. The pleasure of performance is what first attracts children to poetry, the sensual excitement of speaking and hearing the words of the poem." I thank my mother for planting this early seed; it wasn't her fault that it took 20 years to germinate. Maybe, had I been lucky enough to have been raised on a ranch out west where I'd heard some old cowpoke perform poems around a campfire, I'd have become a fan of the language much sooner.

I remember the first time I heard Richard Hugo perform — not simply read, but perform — his poem "Plans for Altering the River." Dick had the knack for giving sometimes long, but never boring introductions to poems and, though I hung closely to his every word, on this occasion, before I realized it, he was already two or three lines into the poem…

> Those who favor our plan to alter the river
> raise your hand. Thank you for your vote.
> Last week, you'll recall…

A bit of fancy footwork? A skosh of showmanship? Surprise! You bet. And why not? Anything to break the cloned reading syndrome ("the title of my next poem is…"). "The only rule," Dick used to say about the writing, "is don't be boring." Sweat runneling horizontally across his furrowed brow, he moved back and forth behind the lab desk in the tiered botany lecture hall. And the lines he recited, without a net, surged through me like a double shot of 190 proof Everclear.

I took it as no mere coincidence, therefore, years later, after Hugo's death and while I was filling in (I use the phrase loosely) for him at the University of Montana, that it was in the same room where I first heard cowboy poetry recited. And no coincidence either that the poet was Wallace McRae, as highly regarded in the Lariati arena as Dick Hugo was in the Literati world. Both poets are Montana institutions, if not heroes, and, now that I closely consider their work side-by-side, their writing harbors very similar sentiments concerning Montana's people and landscapes. And, again, no coincidence that McRae's poems, recited as he paced and strutted behind that large laboratory table, sent that same passionate punch to my solar plexus, that same Hugo-musical delight to my tympanum. No coincidence whatsoever that years after the death of the man who taught me almost everything I know about poetry, and while I still grieved, Wallace McRae should come along and we would strike up a friendship based in large part on our mutual love for Montana, for the land and the language, the latter which Wallace refers to as "the lingo of our calling."

Cowboy poetry — what would Dick Hugo have thought? Doggerel? Something to be ignored or discounted in English wings of universities everywhere? I think not. Not if he'd witnessed an audience of 3,000 strong acknowledging that people's individual lives — in this case, lives that are often rurally isolated — are significant because of the honest emotion invested into, and expressed out of, those lives. He'd have chuckled (not snickered) with delight, I think, at the definition I've coined for cowboy poetry: "the ring and ricochet of lingo off the stirrup bone (stapes) of the middle ear." The truth be known, Dick was not enamored of horses. But I'd bet my kack (saddle) he'd have loved the language of the horseman — reata, latigo, tapadera, concho, hackamore — much of it derived from the Spanish, "the loving tongue," as Charles Badger Clark referred to it in his cowboy poem, "A Border Affair."

All to say, that maybe — just maybe — the overwhelming enthusiastic response to cowboy poetry, by audiences from many walks of life, is in some part due to a non-academic yearning to fulfill a genuine integral need for verse: a need still alive and kicking\bucking\galloping within most of us, a need to hear aloud emotions and ideas conveyed in that good old form, the one most "jagged on the right." In retrospect, I believe I felt this need even as a 16 year-old renegade resisting most everything that had to do with school. I realized that poetry had little, in fact, to do with scholastics. Rather, it was about living life with passion and awareness — which was my mission from the get-go — which was why I think I was a bit stung by poetry's rejection of me.

Obviously, cowboy poetry was not my "savior." (The closest Zimmer came to the subject was a piece titled "Zimmer The Drugstore Cowboy.") Nor am I suggesting that cowboy poetry is the perfect template by which the academic world of verse should be shaped. I'm simply pointing out a few connections and observations, including the fact that two of Gioia's most prominent metaphors are rooted in the rural landscape, both involving agriculture and one of them, most interestingly, set within ten miles of where I make camp here in the Rocky Mountain foothills. "Most editors," he proclaims, "run poems and poetry reviews the way a prosperous Montana rancher might keep a few buffalo around — not to eat the endangered creatures but to display them for tradition's sake...." And a few pages later, "Like subsidized farming that grows food no one wants, a poetry industry has been created to serve the interests of the producers and not the consumers."

The Lariati arena has proven to me that "consumers" are out there and anxious to "buy." Perhaps the Literati could cue to the Lariati's successes in attracting these consumers to "market." If ever poetry, especially on any large scale from the academic world, is going to appeal to regular folks, be they cowboys/cowgirls, fishnetters, engineers, farmers, executives, athletes, mill workers, miners, or what have you, the line drawn — with a D-8 bulldozer built by Rolls Royce — between fine art and folk art is going to have to be narrowed a great deal. To that end, maybe we could be more willing to discuss — especially throughout a reading — or even explain the processes, thoughts, emotions, associations that went into the making of the poem. After reciting one of my more involved pieces in Elko, someone said "you know, I read that poem in your book several times and

I finally decided I didn't like it because it got a little too smoky for me, but your introduction to it tonight made it ring clearer."

Most people expect introductions. The bulk of what they read is journalistic prose, which usually offers a "guiding hand" to lead them into and through the subject matter step by step. Poets, on the contrary, eventually learn that poems tend to begin somewhere in the middle, that the "introduction-body-summary conclusion" rule learned over and over throughout our school years does not apply to verse. When it comes to the rudest side of the ar-tiste, however, to explain is to violate the Code of Artistic Ethics. Years back, my good poet-friend, Verlena Orr, sent me a two-inch-in-diameter lavender pin which reads in bold black letters "FUCK ART — LET'S DANCE." I keep it in eyesight of my writing desk at all times, because, what it says to me is "don't take yourself that seriously."

Thus far, I've discovered only a couple of square feet of common ground between the Literati and the Lariati. However, from this pinnacle overlooking red-rock canyonland laid out like an eye-dazzler Navajo rug — from this vantage point — I've experienced some of the most harmonious, artistically gratifying moments in which my poetry has echoed through an audience. My wish, as is the wish of Dana Gioia (if I read him right), is to nurture this small plot, and to witness it growing until it becomes a large enough "stage" from which most any poet can speak the common language of, and to, the individuals who comprise the masses. And what we should be saying to them, again and again, is "please listen while we acknowledge and pay tribute to (Y)our lives."

It doesn't matter how long you live there
the same waitress will forget
how you like your coffee
but not your men
suntanned and from out of town.
Not one detail escapes her scrutiny,
the brawny hay haulers from Shelley,
the linemen the county hired from Boise
who spun cookies in the snow
on the high school football field
(a federal offense in this town).
She overlooks your black eye
and the scar on your cheek.
You're not seen in town for weeks;
she never asks why.
That doesn't make good conversation
over coffee
after the weather's exhausted
and the economy straightened out.

Penelope Reedy

ANYFIELD; POP. 42

COURTING THE TWO-HEADED SERPENT: WRITING IN THE PROVINCES

BY PENELOPE REEDY

TODAY I RECEIVED a review copy of an anthology of poems by poets of the "inland Pacific Northwest." After browsing through it briefly, I realized how many of these anthologies I've seen these past few years, most of them commemorating Centennial celebrations in various western states. Much of the contemporary work that appears in these books has never before been published, and with good reason; little of it qualifies as "literature" in "legitimate" circles, and that which does must keep company with writers who are included for token political reasons, rather than for the quality of their work. (I knowingly leave myself open for criticism here since my work has been included in a couple of these anthologies.)

Why does it seem natural to editors to lump writers together by regions, drawing odd little geographical boundaries around us as if we're a species of tree indigenous to a few square miles of earth, as if we are rooted and immobile? The truth is we are being classified with terms which are really lead lines in advertising campaigns, cute phrases distinguishing various economic regions. So we have writers (really consumers) of the Pacific Northwest (Seattle), the inter-mountain West (Salt Lake City), the inland Pacific Northwest (Spokane), the inland-Empire (Spokane again), the West Coast (Portland), the Great Basin (Reno?), the Rocky Mountain West (Denver), the High Plains (Denver again), not to mention each individual state, etc., and to complicate it further, we are inundated by a rush of conscience which insists on adding ethnic categories to the hullabaloo: Black Cowboy Poets of the Inter-Mountain West, Native American Poets of the Northwest, Hispanic Cabellero poets of the West Coast, etc.

These nicely printed anthologies are copiously "Prefaced" and "Introduced," and many bear "Afterwords" and Epilogues" in which these writers and their regions are laboriously "explained" to the reader. It's as if there is a fear, and in most cases a justifiable one, that these poems and stories will have no appeal beyond their regions and must therefore be justified to the "outside" world. I was taught that if a cover letter was required to explain a piece of writing to an editor, the piece of writing was probably a failure. If this is so, then why are regional anthology editors forcing these works on us? Why are publishers publishing them?

Well, perhaps publishers are able to make a little money selling these books, and perhaps the reason they make money has more to do with the lack of sophistication among readers in these consumer regions I mentioned, than it does with the philosophies and skills of the writers who happen to live in these areas. From where I sit, it appears that the audiences of such books are made up of the writers themselves and the extended families and friends, as well as a literate, but rather uneducated readership who look for any references to a "history" of their own region, place names with which they can identify, and maybe even a reference to their own family name, nestled among claims of regal larger-than-life almost supernatural archetypical heroes who "won the west."

When perusing these books for germs of literature, I inevitably come across a cliche reminiscence or two and am reminded of my stepfather, a worn and craggy cattleman, who judged any work of art, from painting to novel, by whether or not he figured the artist "knew his horses." I grew up hearing my father and my uncles saying things like, " I don't know anything about poetry, but I know what I like." And I've sat in audiences at the annual Cowboy Poetry Gathering in Elko, Nevada, where a "damned good poet" is one who makes his audience either laugh or cry. There's not much room for subtlety in a medium written almost entirely in anapestic tetrameter quatrains with an ABAB rhyme scheme. If there are too many syllables in a line, the performer simply says them faster to make the words fit. Watching these "cowboys" (and a few of them really are cowboys) in their finery, bright silk scarves tied at their throats, silver conchos, $200 hats, $500 handmade boots, I'm reminded of peacocks preening, but the display isn't for the women as much as it is for each other. Cowboy poetry is a man's world and the women who breech this world do so at their own risk. Hence a few weak cute voices in ruffles whine about their men's neglect, or craggy weathered females tell it like it is to be a "good hand." Real stuff I suppose, but little of it will outlast the gatherings. The "Classic" cowboy poetry has already been written by the like of Bruce Kiskaddon, Wally McRae, and Curly Fletcher. The brief era when it was not only an art form, but a way of dealing naturally with hardships and loneliness on long dry cattle drives is long gone. Yet nowadays in Idaho and Nevada, anyone who has ever sat a horse and can make four lines rhyme thinks he's a poet, thinks he can be a hit at the next gathering. Maybe he can. Books and tapes of the gathering's "poets" seem to sell rather successfully, and Baxter Black, an annual feature, makes his living speaking at Production Credit Association dinners and the like throughout the West, after which he autographs and sells his self-published volumes.

In the provinces, bad, or at best mediocre, fiction and poetry sell. Why? Partly because bad poetry and bad fiction tend to mimic the lie that represents how most people in small communities like to think of themselves. People in small towns, the more rural the better, like to think they are the kindest, most benevolent people in the world. When a writer who knows them well, because he or she was born among them, refuses to project this image, decides instead to paint a more honest, even loving picture, of his community complete with warts and scars, all hell breaks loose. Locals not only refuse to buy such books (or if they do, do so with the intent of examining them for material with which to feed malicious gossip), but ban them in their local libraries and sue the author for such things as defamation of character. A regional publisher takes a great risk when he publishes such literature. The thought of publishing novels with the "strength" of Willa Cather's *My Antonia*, Grace Metalious' *Peyton Place*, Sinclair

Lewis' *Main Street*, Robert McAlmon's *Village*, Sherwood Anderson's *Winesburg, Ohio*, Vardis Fisher's *Toilers of the Hills* would make a western publisher quite nervous these days. As these now well-respected authors found out, through lawsuits and the common rural small-town practice of shunning, there is an emotional price to pay for such honesty. These books sold, however, and in some cases are still selling. Perhaps it was the aura of scandal, the American public's taste for thrills that was responsible for their initial national popularity. It certainly wasn't local or regional gratitude for the attention. These writers are still held suspect in their hometowns. Even though Vardis Fisher has been dead for over twenty years, one still encounters hostility in the provinces over the unflattering, though sympathetic picture he painted of Idaho settlers. And it's interesting to note that Fisher's office mate when he taught at New York University was none other than the province-bred writer, Thomas Wolfe. Wolfe's infamous novel *You Can't Go Home Again*, attests to the difficulty of returning to a place that one has outgrown. And one thing upon which all writers concur is that writing, at least striving to write well, is a growth process.

So, what effect does writing have on both the writer and his community? How have past writers, and writers who are practicing their craft today, cleared paths for the artistic use of their minds? As everyone knows, Hemingway, Fitzgerald, G. Stein, Bryher, Pound, McAlmon, etc., all abandoned their variously small American "uncultured" environments and hung out in London, Paris, Venice, etc., in hopes of tapping into the long established literary traditions of the mother Continent and also to find new perspectives on their own American backgrounds. Perspective seems to be the key here. Can provincial writers who choose to stay close to home overcome the quagmire of public and family opinion in their region? Can a local writer deal effectively with the very real fear of what his mother or the gossipy neighbor might think of his or her less-than-complimentary manuscript?

"You can't say that!" was a common phrase I encountered in the early days of Camas Writer's Workshop, the writing group in Camas County, Idaho, that I initiated in 1975 and that eventually became *The Redneck Review*. I kept asking myself "Why?" Why is it that in a community which claims truth and honesty among its values, that no one had better write the truth without fear of "gettin' run outta town"? Sadly, *The Redneck Review* is no longer published in Camas County and neither does the magazine have a single subscriber from that high mountain valley. Local people lost interest in the magazine as soon as it started showing signs of success, as soon as its editor stopped feeling an obligation to be "nice" (by local definition), and as soon as she began to let "dirty rotten outsiders" publish within its pages.

Just as Vardis Fisher, Willa Cather, Sherwood Anderson, etc., found it necessary to remove themselves from their home communities in order to gain "artistic distance," so it seems contemporary writers in the backwaters of the American West must find solutions to this problem. William Studebaker, a well-known Idaho poet, no longer lives in his hometown of Salmon, Idaho, which is the setting for much of his work, but has adopted instead a slightly more urban environment a couple hundred miles from "home." He doesn't encourage his hometown family and friends to think of him as a writer, and he feels his secret is relatively safe, since most of his work is published in literary magazines which aren't likely to be found on the rack at the local barber shop.

So, the question shifts from "How do writers juggle the demands of their small home communities and remain true to their calling?" to "Are they, in fact, able, for whatever reasons, to stay in the communities upon which their major works are focused?" All the writers I've talked with over the years agree that some form of distance is required in order to be a writer though we've always claimed that such distance can be created "internally" as well as via physical removal from one's environment. Leslie Leek, an excellent Idaho short story writer (her book is *Heart of a Western Woman*, Blue Scarab Press, and is unfortunately out of print at the moment) says that she remembers as a child in Dubois, Idaho, adopting the stance of observer, one who stepped back from live action in order to watch the scenes of her life spread before her as if they were scenes in a movie. She feels that this "internal distance" which she naturally possessed, has been invaluable to her as a writer. She says she doesn't personally feel hostility when she returns for visits to Dubois, yet confesses that her parents have died and she hasn't actually lived in Clark County for many years, specifically the years since she's been publishing. She feels that people on her home turf are mostly not aware of her stories.

Perhaps becoming a writer and remaining in one's community is indeed an impossible combination. In developing this article, I was unable to find a single seasoned, "serious" writer in my region who writes about and continues to live full time in his "Home" community. And from my own experience, having spent the majority of my adult years in Fairfield, Idaho, the community where my father was born and raised, where my grandparents homesteaded, I believe that any writer who wants to continue living in his home town, must keep his work to himself and not talk about anything but the price of hay and the "damned taxes" when he shows up for morning coffee at the local cafe. And if the writer is a woman, she'd better not give evidence of having any "notions," for an adage provincial communities live by is "Ya let a woman out, she gets 'the big head.'" (It would be laughable if it wasn't so sadly true.)

In order to maintain sanity, I would suggest that such writers go to literary conferences in large cities in distant states (They shouldn't tell anyone where they're really going; instead, using an excuse such as the funeral of a distant relative is safer.). There they can met other writers and establish lifeline correspondences (letters which are mailed in thick, tightly sealed plain envelopes to keep local postmasters from suspecting anything). And there too, they can make secret plans to meet again, and afterwards drink beer late into the night, talk about their work, the books they've read, cuss editors' tastes, or best of all, simply delight in the rare camaraderie, because writing in the provinces is a deathly lonely business.

Ideally, after the excitement of being with her own kind, the writer can return refreshed to her simple country house, deserted streets, neighbors who watch her with binoculars, a mailman who holds mail up to the light before putting it in her box, inane conversations about the weather, the same jokes about wives, husbands, virility, mothers-in-law, that remain in the collective unconscious of blue collar coffee klatches the world over, and then one morning, as she sips coffee at the cafe, the waiter leans over the table somewhat provocatively, the light catches his profile in a unique way, a snatch of colorful dialogue wafts across her ear, and she hurries home to the solitude of her house to pound out a new story, new poems, suddenly feeling she's gained a new perspective on the human condition. She contemplates the birth of a new literature that will revolutionize meaning and play a crucial role in the development of civilization.

But, wait, this is fantasy, this "ideal" situation. The reality is I'm moving to Milwaukee.

FRAGMENTS FROM THE SACRED TEXT: THE WRITER'S LIFE AS A SUBJECT

BY SHARON DOUBIAGO

What would happen if one woman spoke the truth? The world would break open.

— Muriel Rukeyser

I HAVE A FILMMAKER friend who says in a hundred years we'll go to the library to check out films on real people. Fiction, make-believe, what we know of now as the movies, will seem primitive and silly.

I AM FIVE, spinning cartwheels under the Los Angeles sky, to the rhythm of the mantra I've learned from Socrates: Know Thyself!

IN THE LAST THING I wrote before I took my vow not to be a poet, a vow I understood then most consciously as having to do with the lying words that created the Vietnam War, I uncovered a repressed story from my childhood so devastating I believed it could kill certain persons. I kept the vow for only six years, 1968 to 1974, but it's taken twenty-two years to get back to the open, vulnerable place of the secret, and the realization that I quit writing to protect not just those persons, but also, to protect the self they had created in me. I quit writing poetry so as not to know myself.

DURING THE TIME of this vow I had a great and beautiful correspondence. Ramona and I exchanged thirty-plus page letters two and three times a week. I began to know a part of myself that can be known only in language. Equally important — in the task of becoming a writer, that is, knowing the reader — I came to know language in her. The word for this alchemy of equal exchange is *Love*.

On November 22, 1975, Ramona's brother killed himself. She asked me to write a poem about it, a request I couldn't refuse. It became my first *real*, completed poem, a first public writing in which I allowed my terrorized unknown self to emerge, and submerge, as deeply into the language as the subject, the occasion, required.

Soon afterwards *My Brother Took His Life November 11, He Tied a Plastic Bag Over His Head* was published in a local paper. The following week a local man killed himself by tying a plastic bag over his head.

I'm standing in the front room of my cabin reading the news story of this man. I see his body, my poem lying beside him. My ears are beginning their old unbearable ringing, my heart to pound, and my sight is going — my Self diminishing within the body, growing smaller and smaller in the deadliest of prisons, the lie pressed upon me since infancy, IT'S YOUR FAULT.

My greatest fear as a writer, that my words will kill if I tell the truth, seemed to come true with my first important publication. But then something happened. A crack began in the fictional world. I didn't faint. I didn't renew my vow. I went to my desk, and in great trepidation and loathing, wrote it out.

Four months later my husband of nine years left me and my children because I had become a poet. His parting words were, "If you write about me, I will come back and kill you."

I knew great compassion for his position and denied, except in the nightmares, my fear and the injustice. I called it the Missing Poem and wrote around the actual story. Years later, on the eve of the publication of my first book, I realized I had weakened my art for his unworthy sake; he still dominated and controlled me. In the most fragile of epiphanies, I finally realized *it's my story, too.*

MORE RECENTLY I had another love who treated me badly. He said this was because I was failing his great love of me. I kept trying. The harder I tried the worse things got — though in a profound way the more I knew love of him.

One summer day his second great love appeared in the garden. I was delighted to meet Beatrice, the beautiful woman in his personal mythology whose power was so great she'd led him from his first wife and infant son. I've always loved my sisters, a fact my men have never believed, or, maybe, trusted.

I am leading her into my studio. Behind me she is saying, I'VE TAKEN A VOW THAT IF I EVER ENCOUNTER AN-OTHER WOMAN LIVING WITH — — — I WILL TELL HER OF THE SISTER SUPPORT GROUP IN HIS NAME.

"Sit down," she said then, gently, indicating my typewriter. "I'm going to dictate the Sisters' message to you.

> *"First, this is who you are: a powerful, independent, creative, erotic, woman, who loves men, who still believes in love. This, you must know, is a description of all the sisters, the two dozen I've been meeting with for years. He doesn't know this about himself, it is not that he is malefic, but a malefic force is in him in regards to women. He is attracted to the most powerful women so he can destroy them. In this destruction he finds what he thinks is his manhood.*
>
> *"Second, this is what is going to happen to you."*

I typed it out, the Sisters' itinerary for me. A year and a half later, through the worst betrayal yet — partly because I was convinced I had learned the lesson — I went searching for this writing. When I found it, I held in my hands the exact story I had just lived, right down to the very sentence with which he had kicked me out. *"You're no longer erotic to me."*

THE IMMORALITY OF exposing a loved one, one with whom one has had the sacred experience of *knowing*, is perhaps my largest understanding. I've always called this Love, and quoted Rilke: " *The role of the lover is to protect the privacy of the loved one."* My journey has been to see that this cosmic law has not been reciprocated for me, that my soul has not been protected by the ones who vowed to do this. Now I come back to my childhood secret, but my love is not less. Now I search for the true balance, my betrayals and theirs, of unconditional love. Now I know it is the Goddess holding the Scales of Love who is blindfolded, not either of the lovers.

"WHAT ABOUT YOUR private life?" a guy asked me tonight at The Mark Antony. "I admit I've been fascinated by you, I've watched you a lot. But you won't like what I see." He told me anyway. "You have about fifteen veils." His hand indicated them before his face.

"Veils are okay," I responded. "You can take off veils. They're soft, erotic. The Goddess wears veils."

Before the conversation took this hostile turn, he'd told me of his nascent efforts to be a poet and asked me about when I accepted the calling, if it was hard. Now this question fell together with the one of my private life.

"It was the hardest thing I've ever done. I accepted my calling at the precise moment I understood that as a private person I would always be betrayed by the man I love. I accepted it when I understood that my unconditional love was tipping the Scales. I accepted it rather than give up my faith that there are men capable of love, that there is a man I can love who can love me. I went public with my soul, my most private self, as a way of making the world make me accountable for something I am not strong enough to do alone. I went public as part of the Sister Support Group — we, the Great Ones, who, despite everything, still believe there are Great Men."

I wasn't wrong in 1968 about Vietnam. War begins in the Lover's bed, in the House where Father is King. I just didn't know myself.

A.B. GUTHRIE RETROSPECTIVE

BY DOUG MARX

READING A.B. GUTHRIE'S *The Big Sky* this summer — justly thought of as the definitive "mountain man" novel — fretful about this article, I kept wondering what my wife, often sitting near me, hugely round and radiantly fed-up in her ninth month, would think of such a book. "Get a load of this," I jibed, barely eight pages into the story — by which time its focus, a young Boone Caudill, had already beat-up one guy and been sucker-punched by his own Pap as punishment, an act of guidance that inspires the lad to coldcock the old man with a club, whence he says good-bye to his Ma and lights out for the West from his Kentucky home: "Boone figured that he hadn't done anything that a true man wasn't bound to do. A man couldn't look himself in the face if he let people make little of him. What if he did have some store liquor in him when he tackled Mose? It was still right, and it settled things man to man."

My efforts at conversation were met with much eye-rolling and a suggestion to keep the book's remaining "man to man" passages to myself. Under different circumstances, I might have mischievously ignored her advice, breaking the languorous quiet of our sunny afternoons with "Listen to this!" gleefully reciting again and again: "A true man does this, a real man does that." And I could have, easily, because this phraseology comes up a lot in Guthrie's novels of the Old West, irrespective of the good, bad and ugly characters being referred to.

Tactlessly recounting these hours of domestic bliss, I don't mean to make fun of Guthrie's genuine achievement as a writer, nor to signal some tirade to follow, charging him with historical war crimes in the so-called battle of the sexes. What's important are the documents themselves, what, if anything, they have to say to us now, that we might understand ourselves and change for the better. That's why, I suppose, about halfway through *The Big Sky*, I looked at my wife with a nod and a wink and said: "You know, if that's a son you're carrying, you really ought to read this book. At least you'll know what you're up against — the deep historical sources and social and cultural perspectives that inform everything from the "wimp factor" to bumperstickers that read: MY WIFE YES, MY DOG MAYBE, MY GUN NEVER or HUNTERS GO DEEPER INTO THE BUSH AND EAT WHAT THEY KILL."

I WANT TO DIGRESS for a moment, if only to make some broad generalizations and give some odd personal and historical context to what will eventually follow.

Thinking about Guthrie, who passed away in April 1991, I try to imagine his more than 40 years of work: five big novels about the Old West, several mysteries, a book of short stories, autobiographical writings, a children's book and, just recently, a collection of essays that stand as tribute to his long-term environmental concerns. *The Big Sky*, his first novel, published in 1947, was followed by its 1950 Pulitzer Prize-winning sequel, *The Way West*, which gave us, once-for-all, a dramatic picture of life on the Oregon Trail. *These Thousand Hills* (1956) extended the view into the ranching days of the 1880s, and *Fair Land, Fair Land* — a book I find inferior, like a parody of a John Wayne/ Gabby Hayes screenplay, director John Ford notwithstanding — completed *The Big Sky* series in 1981, tying up loose ends.

I think back to 1947. Here's an American writer, born in Indiana, raised in Choteau, Montana, the state he leaves for 20 years to attend Harvard and work as a journalist in Kentucky, returning home to spend the last half of his life telling the story of the Old West. World War II is just over. Auschwitz and the Bomb are historical facts.

As to artistic and literary milieu, during the years in which Guthrie works on *The Big Sky*, Gertrude Stein dies, Malcomb Cowley saves William Faulkner's career with his *The Portable Faulkner*, Pound is institutionalized — and in Europe the existentialists, led by Sartre, are making themselves heard. *Film noir* has everybody going with a kind of urban, mid-20th century lone wolf known as a private dick. Abstract Expressionism has taken over New York. *The Big Sky* appears the same year Willa Cather dies, and doesn't appear on a list of "significant" fiction that includes novels by Bellow, Vidal, Dreiser, Steinbeck, Stafford and a dozen others unremembered by us now. Mailer's *The Naked and the Dead* comes out a year later.

So here's Guthrie out in the middle of nowhere writing about mountain men. I haven't the foggiest what — if any — historical connection he might have drawn between his tragic heroes and the national character of the most powerful country on earth. What I do feel is that these books — which are as dark and tragic in their human implications as they are celebratory of the wilderness — lay out for all to see the fundamental perversions in our cultural notions about such words as "liberty" and "freedom," and the way those perversions infect and contradict our ideas about community.

IN HIS INTRODUCTORY essay to *The Big Sky,* Walter Van Tilburg Clark, author of *The Ox-Bow Incident,* goes on at some length trying to understand why the mountain man never found his rightful place in our pantheon of American heroes. His remarks begin: "This is a book about a mountain man, and if American mythmaking had followed anything like the true ancient pattern, the mountain man would certainly be our number one Hero by now."

Baffled by the staying power in the popular imagination of such heroes as the backwoodsman and the cowboy, Clark (writing in 1964) nearly opens a vein in his determination to save the mountain man from folkloric extinction. In the end, scorning cowboys as imposters on mountain-man pedestals, ridiculing a "lady" — and "using that appellation in its least winning sense" — for her prudish, bluestocking rejection of Boone Caudill as an heroic type, Clark offers a couple of historical and anthropological explanations. First, lasting barely a generation, the mountain man adventure was a cultural dead-end, coming to a close in the mid-19th century; and, second, their relative illiteracy, together with survival habits such as "covering their tracks," left them as ghosts without a proper mythmaking foundation. "[This] state of things can't last," Clark complains in his last paragraph, adding: "Only Heroes born in verity can give a nation a soul, and only Heroes who give a nation a soul can find a place in its enduring pantheon."

As it happens — and though I agree with him that the cowboy is a monstrous cultural fake who couldn't walk a mile in a mountain man's moccasins — I can't share in Clark's dismay for the way mountain men have been given short shrift as national soul-makers. I do, however, believe that there is a great deal to be learned from *The Big Sky* about ourselves as a nation, and that it behooves us to understand just what those lessons suggest.

None of this is to imply that Guthrie, writing one of the great tragic books of the American experience, romanticized his history. It is, after all, nothing less than a secularized *Paradise Lost*. Nor does Boone Caudill, a veritable cave man, serve as his paradigmatic man's man. Dick Summers, Caudill's surrogate father and the central figure of both *The Way West* and *Fair Land, Fair Land*, plays that Adamic role. Also included in Guthrie's gallery of mountain men are easy-going Jim Deakins, Caudill's best friend and opposite, who will play Abel to his Cain; Caudill's Uncle Zeb; and Summers' sidekick, Higgins, a good old coot with a twinkle in his eye and a toothless hoot for a laugh.

However various these men and the range of values they embody as characters, they have in common one attitude that overarches the differences between them with regard to their thoughts and feelings about, say, women, or Indians or God. These men are all loners to the bone. If not anti-social, then asocial. Some, like Caudill, are born losers whose rage verges on misanthropy.

These men didn't head west out of some noble sense of exploration, to endure and exalt in the unknown, to make maps of the wilderness, plant flags and bring the booty home to their sovereign. Which is but one of the reasons why they will never be popular heroes to the herd. They were all fleeing, leaving the herd and its duties, laws and responsibilities behind, lighting out for some vast mountain range where they might not see a human face for months. Sure, some of them had heard of the land's immensity and were drawn to it, but most, like Caudill, were running away from home and the human race.

This is a feeling no doubt common to many, but for most it remains a feeling only. For a brief moment in North American history, a few men had an opportunity to go to the wilderness and become a kind of weird white Noble Savage. Alone in the mountains, living by their wits, mountain men measured concepts such as "freedom" and "liberty" in proportion to their distance from anyone else. Distance measured in miles. Two was company — maybe — three a crowd. Unfortunately, freedom and liberty have no meaning when their context comes down to one person, which is the result of the logic of the "real man" pushed to its conclusion.

That meaninglessness is tragically ruinous, as Caudill's murder of his best friend shows. For a wiser man, such as Summers, the tragedy lies in the knowledge of the destruction of the wilderness and the native peoples who lived there, and the self-knowledge that he had a hand in it. (*Fair Land, Fair Land* falls apart when Summers, years later, because a man's gotta do what a man's gotta do, tracks Caudill down and provokes him, at which point Higgins steps in to blow Caudill away, not only saving Summers' life, but also putting him beyond reach of the possibility of having that kind of blood on his hands.)

Freedom, liberty, individualism, it boggles the brain to imagine a map of this country, late 1830s, with the mountain men in Montana trapping beaver, living an uneasy coexistence with the Indians, and, say, Thoreau in his hut by Walden Pond, a cranky Yankee philosophizing about the relationship of the individual to society.

Walter Van Tilburg Clark's concerns about the mountain man's lack of historical influence to the side, it's my hunch that our national infatuation with cowboys and their Wild West codes of liberty and justice reveals that the mountain men are very much alive and with us. There are, for instance, deep shades of Guthrie's favorite character, Dick Summers, in a cowboy like *Shane,* played by Alan Ladd in the classic film, one of several that Guthrie, a Hollywood enthusiast, helped write. Ironically, the character of Shane is one of the archetypal "cowboy[s] on the pedestal" that so infuriated Clark in the 1960s.

But enough of using Clark as an innocent foil. The point is, though the mountain men might not be with us as folk heroes on a level with, say, Daniel Boone — who was an Elks Club kind of guy — a great deal of their ethos does. Cowboy consciousness is the loner with no place else to go, returned to drift the peripheries of family and town, still settling things man to man, quite often at somebody else's expense. Somewhere along the line it seems that the macho mystique of that lone-wolf individualism became the real-life code of people doomed to live elbow to elbow. It haunts us every day in the violent social nightmare we see out the window or watch on TV. It's an individualism that has no feel for teamwork or cooperation, which just doesn't work in a mass society.

Guthrie knew this. He also knew that his mountain men, from Caudill to Summers, were failures in damn near all ways but one and that's their struggle to survive in the wilderness — the true hero of Guthrie's books. The trails they cut and the mountain passes they discovered became the wagon ruts that sealed their extinction and accelerated the destruction of the land. A couple of times recently, I've flashed on an image of Guthrie alive and driving, maybe following a full-load log truck that coughs black smoke into the air, staring at a license plate that says Big Sky.

I don't know how Guthrie might have felt about somebody half his age stepping in to point out a connection between the values and attitudes his "real men" embrace in their pursuit of freedom and independence, and the wreckage they inevitably leave in their wake. Yet, how he might have felt doesn't matter: exhaustively researched, fully imagined, painfully honest, his novels of the Old West read like casebook studies of the roots of one of the fundamental problems of this society, as when people start shooting guns at one another on the freeway.

This is a rich legacy. And the writing?

"Boone yelled something to him, and Summers shook his head, and Boone cupped his hands around his mouth and yelled again, but sound wouldn't come against the wind; it blew backward down the pass, and Summers found himself wondering how far it would blow until it died out and was just one with the rush of air."

SCIENCE FICTION AND FANTASY

BY GREG BEAR

SPEAKING TO A GOOD friend recently, I came to a sudden realization that the war had been won. Science fiction and fantasy have permeated the world consciousness; past discriminations against the literature we love have fled. What few backwaters of literary bigotry remain are rather like those countries still wrapped in the shroud of Stalin and Mao — poor, depressed, deeply in trouble.

Our conversation went like this: he read me the lyrics of a song for a Broadway musical for which he's writing the book, a musical rife with science fiction elements and brisk references to science fiction lore; we talked about a review of one of my books in *People* magazine; we discussed science fiction and fantasy's regular appearance in the Book-of-the-Month Club; Poland and the Soviet Union are now paying cash U.S. dollars for American science fiction; and so on.

The war's over. It's time to get on with the peace. And the peace means writing with every tool at our disposal, writing as passionately as we can, to reach that large and eclectic audience of readers who, whether they know it or not, are ripe for the very best science fiction and fantasy.

There's one catch. More bad science fiction and fantasy are being written now than ever before. The popularity of these genres — if indeed they are genres, having few if any limitations of style and form — has attracted thousands of beginners with no previous experience, or hacks with no passion or love.

Publishers, fighting for lucrative rack space, have published thousands of terrible books. The amount of bad or mediocre science fiction and fantasy published now is astonishing, more than ever before. Some of it makes best-seller lists; some of it even wins prestigious awards. Most of it doesn't begin to approach the top of the form.

Science fiction and fantasy are the hardest kinds of literature to write well. They require not just a keen eye and a sharp prose style, but a wild imagination and education in areas as diverse as science and technology, history, comparative religions, linguistics, musicology…an apprenticeship in either field could take ten or fifteen years, just to achieve minimal competence, let alone excellence.

Let's start at the beginning: what is science fiction? The name is established, unavoidable, and not completely misleading. It is fiction that uses science's ideal world-view of selfless objectivity to tell timeless stories dealing with the deep nature of existence, consciousness, organization, humanity, life. Science fiction is not limited by what the writer has personally experienced, though that will inevitably shape the writer's fictions. It is not limited by religion, culture, or even by the present laws of science. Its only limitation — more a liberation, actually — is its demand that the writer, and the reader, step outside of their selves and see through other eyes, in other spaces, places, and times. It demands extraordinary empathy for otherness, not just Milton's sympathy for Satan, but an awareness of the character and importance of all beings human and otherwise, real and potential. Prejudice should be its antithesis; discovery its only fixed law.

Good science fiction is not just good literature; it's exercise for the marathon future.

Fantasy is more inner-directed, past-oriented. Fantasy explores the subconscious in more traditional modes. Religion, history, and language heavily color fantasy; science is less important, though not negligible. Fantasy has its own kind of freedom. Both modes are rich and important. And good fantasy is no easier to write than good science fiction, though with our present state of education, it may be more accessible to more writers and readers than science fiction.

Why do I concentrate on science fiction? The strictures of the sf fugue appeal to me. The discipline expands my art. I do not start with the strictures: my mind runs free, examining a wide range of dreamlike possibilities. I then ask myself, how can the scientific world-view allow these things to *be?* And I find in them the problems and emotions that most intrigue and puzzle me. I work using both subject and story structure to get beneath the reader's skin, to grab the reader's heart and mind simultaneously.

Science fiction has a reputation for cold rationality, but that's a misconception. At the heart of science fiction, as well as science, is the mystic urge for transcendence, for growth and survival, love and appreciation.

Personal example: my most recently published novel, *Queen of Angels,* is set some sixty years from today, in Los Angeles and Haiti. Its subject is sanity and self-awareness, both personal and cultural, explored through the plot elements of mass murder, political turmoil, and psychological therapy. Its infrastructure includes nanotechnology — the as-yet theoretical technology of very small organic machines — and a new kind of psychological investigation into the Country of the Mind. It is uncompromising in its language, suggesting the patois and syntax of 2047–48. Its literary structure is a series of handball reverberations that build to solutions as the book progresses, through at least three levels of metaphor. Four very different main characters let us see the world through their eyes; the central character, black poet Emanuel Goldsmith, appears only briefly in person, but his spirit — and his madness — haunts the book and gives it its shape.

I leave it to readers to decide whether the book succeeds; what I mean to suggest is that science fiction writers, to reach the top of the form, should command an array of techniques and information that would dazzle past masters in and out of science fiction.

At the same time, for me, story is supreme; story-telling is the spine of my work. I hope, through science fiction and fantasy, to quietly steal into the reader's house and rearrange the furniture, maybe even redecorate; occasionally, demolish and rebuild.

If that's a manifesto, so be it.

It's also a challenge. There's more *excellent* science fiction and fantasy being written now than every before, and the best is truly astonishing. Many of the world's finest writers make science fiction their home. We stand on the shoulders of giants, competing with extremely talented friends, and our audience is the best and the brightest.

That defines a renaissance.

WILLIAM STAFFORD REVISITED

BY DOUG MARX

HAVING MET WILLIAM STAFFORD just a couple of times, I know him mostly by his books, public image and the kind of chit-chat that goes down when literary types get together. In these respects I've known him a long while. Half my life, now that I think of it. Over 20 years ago, just beginning to read poems, I came upon the lines: "Traveling through the dark I found a deer/dead on the edge of the Wilson River road," and my head snapped back in recognition. I knew that stretch of highway like a walk to the store, and I'd been there on the shoulder, heartsick, rolling a car-crippled doe into the canyon. I didn't know what a National Book Award was, nor that Stafford was all the rage. What I did know was that I was hungry to have that kind of bookish experience again, which led to an addiction I've never been able to kick.

So much for my "revisiting" Stafford. The thought that I ought to work up some kind of scholarly overview that provides for a new understanding of his work gives me the creeps. What makes me shudder even more is that, having taken this assignment, the deadline devil whispers in my ear: "Go ahead, make it easy on yourself, slip them another 'What Stafford Means to Me' essay. Nobody will know the difference."

I've been known to take that kind of advice, duty bound to the first principle of free-lancing (feed thy face), but in this case, sitting down to write about Stafford, all I come up with are notions about what he *doesn't* mean to me. Somehow, after years of reading his poems and listening to people talk about them, the poet I have in mind is the opposite of the one who lives in the popular imagination — another Frost, Sandburg or Williams, a "poet of the people" (as one jacket blurb calls him), whose simple words, rich in wisdom, transcend the complexity of existence.

For instance, it's my subjective perception that lots of people think of Stafford as a spokesperson of consolation, or maybe even hope. Sitting in the audience at a Stafford reading, I always get the feeling that his poetry — perhaps by virtue of its soft, assonantal, cooing vocabulary and seemingly effortless, slack lines — *soothes* people, that they come away from the experience feeling *lifted* and inspirited, as if this enigmatic gnome-like man with owlish eyebrows had just patted them on the head and said: "Hey, still your fears, little one, dry your tears, don't be frightened, it's *okay*."

Which isn't how I feel at all. Reading his poems, hearing them read, looking for the sense beneath their susurrations, I always feel as if I've been touched, if not by despair, then at least by an irremediable sadness more heartbreak than rage, a realization of hopelessness no bucolic evocation of provincial decency can ease.

Stafford's poems come at me like a summer breeze aswarm with stinging yellowjackets. If the warm currents sometimes bore me with the aw-shucks sheepishness of their lullaby — like folk music when I want jazz — still I never nod off, bitten awake by lines as direct and merciless as the hard facts of our condition they convey: "And if we purify the pond, the lilies die."

This kind of talk is more than the remark of a flip dualist. It has about it the symbology of a religious moralist who understands that evil is inescapable. (In a strange way, Stafford writes like Emerson and thinks like Thoreau.) Evil is given a face in his work, it festers in a poem such as "Quiet Town," palpably and without irony.

I don't mean to be heavy-handed. The proof is everywhere in the poems, regardless of the God-talk, ecumenical overtones and appeals to faith, the pep-talks for the meek and gentle who, as Stafford would have it, are better off dissolving into thin air. Stafford might write: "By believing, you can get there"; but I'm not convinced the experience is real for him. The poems say otherwise. Here's the conclusion to "Some Shadows":

> Forgive me these shadows I cling to, good people,
> trying to hold quiet in my prologue.

Hawks cling the barrens wherever I live.
The world says, 'Dog eat dog.'

The first six poems alone in *Traveling Through the Dark,* his first book, read like a poet's casebook of existential dread. There's the absurd but necessary presumption of universal moral accountability in the title poem ("I thought hard for us all") — and again in "Thinking for Berky," which concludes with an indictment as lacerating as Baudelaire's "You, hypocrite lecteur!"

We live in an occupied country, misunderstood;
justice will take us millions of intricate moves.
Sirens will hunt down Berky, you survivors in your beds
listening through the night, so far and good.

"In Medias Res," which doubles as the title of the book's first section, finds a locale in limbo, while connecting personal and social failures with the siege of Troy, which is another way of saying our common plight hasn't improved in 3500 years. "With My Crowbar Key" provides all the Cartesian vertigo and metaphysical bewilderment one needs in a world that, impenetrable, validating nothing, can never be more than "possible."

It's hateful to pigeon-hole poems so glibly, but to me these themes of fear and trembling underlie all of Stafford's work and serve as the testing ground for the side of him that calls for patience, ambiguity, mystery, integrity of selfhood, wilderness and an effort to "locate ourselves by the real things/we live by." "The world speaks everything to us./It is our only friend," Stafford claims in "Allegiances," reiterating the notion in "A Message from Space": "Everything that happens is the message:.../Everything counts. The message is the world." (Remember, from above, that "The world says 'dog eat dog.'")

There's a symbolist streak in Stafford — Baudelaire, again, comes to mind with "Correspondences" — but he knows most of us find that rebus indecipherable, or are too blind to read it, and that even the luckiest never get more than a momentary "twinge" of dubious insight. And *that,* finally, as he puts it in "Knowing," doesn't suffice: "Your hand can make the sign — but begs for/more than can be told: even the world/can't dive fast enough to know that other world."

Not by a long shot the first, Stafford is tormented by this epistemological business of "knowing." It wouldn't be so bad, perhaps, if he weren't also a moralist, which demands discrimination, judgment and logic. He'd like it to be otherwise, "all the while knowing/by living, though not knowing how to live." Yet, what is a moral life in the amoral world of realpolitik? The brain wants an answer to questions about the human condition that the heart can't supply, no matter how it cries out for the primacy of "touch," understanding and the intuitive hunch.

An Epiphany

You thinkers, prisoners of what will work:
a dog ran by me in the street one night,
its path met by its feet in quick unthought,
and I stopped in a sudden Christmas, purposeless,
a miracle without proof, soon lost.

But I still call, "Here, Other, Other," in the dark.

That's Stafford, asking forgiveness for his "shadows" again, as if to say "Sorry to set you up, but death makes a realist of me." If wisdom and understanding are his goals, they have little to do with God, but rather with getting by in this world as undamaged as possible. He's a poet who, for all his deceptive shadowplay and desire to disappear — "I'm no one" — can't leave the actual world, coming across as a Stoic who lives in a time when the traditional refuges of Nature and self have become obsolete.

Again, there's no question that Stafford is a writer of diverse themes. But whether he's talking about family, the value of reticence and the certainty of a "truth" that "didn't care how it came," or the "Bonuses" of *Passwords*, my gut-level feeling is that these heartening aspects of his work amount to a kind of hope against hope that not even the poet himself believes in. As values, they're all "maybes," as in *Someday, Maybe,* that "possible" time in the future for which we might prepare ourselves in the here and now. Or in these lines from "Practice":

Maybe it is all rehearsal, even when practice
ends and performance pretends to happen in the light
that remembers more than it touches, back through all
the rows and balcony tiers. Maybe your stumbling
saves you, and that sound in the night is more than the
    wind.

Well, yes, maybe it is. Then again, maybe it isn't. For now, in Stafford's poems, it's the latter that holds for me, even though he lets his generosity of spirit make it seem otherwise, *for our sakes*. How else explain this confession from a man writing a letter to the sky?: "Toward the last I was protecting my friends by my careful indifference. Oh, I greeted them, and acted as usual, but I didn't let on what I felt — that terrible tide of knowing that came to me." Or this, from *An Oregon Message*, which finds the twin themes of the crisis of belief and knowledge still in full swing 25 years after they were first given form in *Traveling through the Dark*:

> Friends, if you knew what I'm talking about
> you would be glad that I didn't tell you.

That's pretty cold comfort. Grim, in fact. And typical. It's more than abstract philosophy, as well, because what's left unsaid is everything: Life is hard and then you die. And no possibility, no might happen, no maybe can escape that fact, no matter how sweetly put, though song can ease the going.

For me, the William Stafford who is read and viewed as some kind of sylvan spirit, a shy country bumpkin or reincarnated Indian, or as a "poet of the people" burnishing the wood of the "American grain" just doesn't exist. To my experience, I don't think he gives voice to problems that concern the average citizen of this country, no matter how much he might speak in the language of family albums and other populist trappings. Ours is a mechanical, coldly pragmatic culture, not a metaphysical one, and I suspect Stafford's relation to it has him "feeling 'bout as local as a fish in a tree," as an old song tells it. Furthermore, as a lifelong pacifist, Stafford is complete warp in "the American grain," inasmuch as those words say something about our national character and murderous history. (Frost was a patriot who often yearned to participate in affairs of State, whereas Stafford tries to be apolitical.) Love the landscape though he might, wild things, talk to Vergil as he might, he knows our Rome is that of Caligula, not Augustus.

Reading Stafford, it's not Whitman or Frost or Williams who come to my mind, but rather someone like Leopardi — deeply alienated and pessimistic, of a sensibility neither classic nor romantic. Or Czeslaw Milosz, whose work, too, can generally be read as a record of the civil war between the intuitive, spiritual side of himself and the claims of history and reason, which pop like soap bubbles everything he can't help but dream or hope. This is a battle shared by many, but what Stafford and Milosz do as writers is embody and give form to their "possibles" and "maybes" with music and images, while what they say denies it all as fast as they can write it down.

For all that, I don't think Stafford is as God-wracked as Milosz. I think the "possible" his poems long for could be called belonging. It's not the innocence of the child or the "primitive" that he longs for — for neither are "innocent" at all — but rather their presumed integration with the world. Here's a passage from the historian Morris Berman's *The Reenchantment of the World* that seems especially suited to Stafford:

"The view of nature which predominated in the West down to the eve of the Scientific Revolution was that of an enchanted world. Rocks, trees, rivers, and clouds were all seen as wondrous, alive, and human beings felt at home in this environment. The cosmos, in short, was a place of *belonging*. A member of this cosmos was not an alienated observer of it but a direct participant in its drama. His personal destiny was bound up with its destiny, and this relationship gave meaning to his life. This type of consciousness...involves merger, or identification, with one's surroundings, and bespeaks a psychic wholeness that has long since passed from the scene...."

Stafford knows what has "passed from the scene." He knows that the "old ways," however true or quaintly nostalgic, are lost forever to the past, try as he might to make them work again. He's a man for whom starlight, though it takes the breath away, illuminates only the void. Closing one of Stafford's books, grateful for his honesty, understanding his need to soften its sorrow with song, I come away thinking there's nothing left but pity, victims as we all are of that "inexhaustible inheritance," our "Pride and Ignorance."

GETTING THROUGH TO WILLIAM GIBSON

BY JOHN DOMINI

WILLIAM GIBSON — the author of *Neuromancer* among other enormously successful novels and short stories, the man behind a sort-of science-fiction approach clumsily labeled "cyberpunk," the imagination that gave us a darkly glimmering future in which marginal urban hustlers live by their wits in the jaws of corporate-minded rapacity and joust with heroic resourcefulness across a vast computer databank called "cyberspace" — seems by and large an affable guy. He lives in Vancouver, B.C., a corner of the continent famously easy on the nerves. Now 44, he's got two children and a solid marriage. In interview I found him genial, hardworking, and open-minded.

But if ours was a typical Q & A, God help the profession. Gibson and I suffered communications breakdowns rarely seen this side of the Marx Brothers. We had timing problems, technology problems. When I wasn't noting down the man's latest snatch of insight or provocation, I was tearing my hair out over some snafu that prevented my getting more.

For the literal-minded, the trouble's easy to explain. Gibson had changing publicists, pressing deadlines; I had a lousy mic on my tape recorder. Myself, however, I see another shape in all this — a metaphor. Two people who wanted to talk were frustrated by the machinery designed to help. Two voices were lost in cyberspace...

Q: Can something worthwhile have made it across the scrambled wires? Can intelligence fly free of the anomic blur?

A: For every problem, there's a solution.

Problem #1: Definition

Gibson was contracted to do *Neuromancer*, his first novel, on the basis of stories in science fiction magazines like *Omni*. The book then swept the awards for sci-fi: the Hugo, the Nebula, and the Philip K. Dick. And many of the events cluttering his calendar, while we were trying to talk, were what the fans call "sf cons," science fiction conventions.

Yet Gibson refused to think of himself as a science fiction writer. He felt strongly that his entire cyberspace threesome — the first book was followed by *Count Zero* and *Mona Lisa Overdrive* — had found a very different readership.

"Mine is a reverse-science-fiction market," he claimed. "I always saw my work as a *reaction* to what was happening. It goes right up against the conservatism of the early '80s, the cultural Reaganism. And I mean, I saw rank and file science fiction as part of the problem. It's just so conservative, *terribly* conservative."

Gibson's own spell of sf fandom took place in his early teens. "That's the age," he said, "when you're 13 or 14. Myself, by the time I'd hit 17, I'd pretty much rejected the whole genre." He laughed. "All of a sudden I'd realized how simple it was."

When the contract for *Neuromancer* brought him back to this kind of storytelling, it made Gibson uneasy. "A lot of what readers found so multileveled and action-packed about that book came right out of my insecurity about what I found myself doing. I was terrified that people wouldn't want to keep turning pages." He came up with something "constructed on a B-movie armature." But if *Neuromancer* ever became a movie, he added, it wouldn't work as ordinary science fiction. "The costs of the effects alone would require that it be something else altogether.

"I mean," he went on, "mainstream science fiction is basically utopian. It's about solving some temporary problem that's messing up a situation that's basically utopian. My stuff's a lot dirtier and more complex. It's not America-first, either. People jack in from all over the globe."

The Difference Engine bears out Gibson's claims. Co-authored with his friend Bruce Sterling, the new novel makes science fiction of historical fiction; it imagines the ramifications if the computer had been invented in Victorian England. Gibson said that the villains in the book — cutthroat 19th century capitalists — were in fact the kind he'd always imagined for his work.

"My baddies," he told me, "have always been closer to the Victorian 'cracksman' than to anything more cutting-edge."

None of which is to say that Gibson doesn't appreciate what sf has done for him. "It's given me very broad exposure," he admitted. "Much more exposure, I'm sure, than the sort of science fiction I used to read. I mean, most of the time I find that the people who buy my books are pretty satisfying as readers. They may come to me because of the 'science fiction' label, but they see past that quick enough."

He even maintains a certain respect for what he learned at the conferences he went to as a teenager. "I learned that writers were individual people," he said. "It's important to understand that — that they've each got their own address and phone number and credit cards. They're *individuals*...."

Problem #2: Criticism

Gibson took pains to make sure he wasn't perceived as a scholar. "I had whatever passes for a literary upbringing in this culture," he said. "Nothing particularly remarkable." Yet some of his sharpest insights arose from literary talk. All I had to do was mention the three authors to whom critics have most often compared him — Philip K. Dick, Raymond Chandler, and Thomas Pynchon.

Dick (the author died in 1977) is a science fiction touchstone, credited with inventing the run-down yet technofied future (sometimes called dystopia) that Gibson explores in his trilogy. The most famous images of that future are from the 1982 movie *Blade Runner*, in which 21st-century Los Angeles appears as an Arab marketplace framed in naked steel, and *Blade Runner* was adapted from Dick's novel *Do Androids Dream of Electric Sheep?*

"But Dick's not my idea of a model," Gibson insisted. "Not at all."

"The earlier author had a very different morality," Gibson said. "A lot of what I find inspiring," he pointed out, "Dick seems to have found terrifying. His work is a kind of outcry against things like the '60s drug culture or the spread of technology. But when I consider those aspects in our civilization, I see a lot to admire. I mean, if we hadn't had a drug culture, I'd've lost half my metaphors."

He laughed, "Dick was really working through personal problems. I'm basically *happy*, doing my stuff. I keep it at arm's length."

Raymond Chandler likewise leaves him cold. "He's just not that important to me," Gibson said. "I only know a couple of the books, and I mean, the plots are simply preposterous. They're hung on impossible coincidences." If he must be compared to a hard-boiled detective novelist, Gibson would prefer it was Chandler's forerunner. "Dashiell Hammett was by far finer," he told me. "Anyone who wants to see a bizarre urban world, in scintillating detail, all tied to a story you can't get out of your mind — they should look at Hammett."

Gibson at least agreed that Thomas Pynchon had been an influence. "I admire how Pynchon lines up all these losers and cranks," he said, "these marginal figures, and then by the end of the story has them find their own way of fighting the very same powers that have kept them out of the loop. I'd like to think I do something like that...."

But regarding Pynchon too, Gibson resisted the notion of any direct connection. When I compared *Neuromancer's* plot to that of *Gravity's Rainbow*, he objected, "I don't think anyone can say what the plot is in *Gravity's Rainbow*."

Rather than accepting the chums that critics have picked for him, Gibson preferred his own company. "Do you know Nelson Algren's *The Man with the Golden Arm?*" he asked. "That's much closer to what I'm doing. Anybody who gives the opening pages of *Neuromancer* a careful going over is bound to see *The Man with the Golden Arm*." Later he brought up Hunter Thompson. "I've just got to work his name in somewhere. He's meant so much to me."

Critics have done worse than misread Gibson's influences. Some have attacked him as hopeless, an imagination too grim to bear, and some are angry about the lack of politically correct figures in his books, the lack of women role models especially. The author has addressed both criticisms many times by now. During our conversations he talked about these issues affably as ever — but also swiftly, dismissively.

"That kind of thinking," he said, "is exactly what I mean when I say most science fiction is essentially conservative. Some people just don't want you to make up any kind of future, not really. I think of myself as working with what's already the reality. I just take it a step or two in certain directions.

"Now women's rights, for instance," he went on, "in the cyberspace books women's rights haven't moved either forward or back. They're just hanging in more or less where they are now. Personally I'd prefer it otherwise, I mean I was just shocked when the Equal Rights Amendment didn't pass, but my story's somewhere else. My story needs that grounding in a here and now that's not too different from our own."

Gibson also pointed out that *Mona Lisa Overdrive* has a bona-fide heroine. Mona has worked as a prostitute (selling out is a theme in the book) and the author acknowledged that "some people might not find her background acceptable. But," he insisted, "she's put herself together by the end of the story. She's a strong character."

Beyond that, Gibson didn't much care to defend his work. The replies to his critics took off after stranger pursuits; without warning he'd move on to a computer game he'd seen recently.

"It's called Sim City," he said. "You know I've always liked video games, they were part of the inspiration for cyberspace…."

Problem #3: Place

A writer is more than his genre, more than his reviews. He's also, as Gibson put it, a person with an address and phone number — with a shaping place. Gibson spoke affectionately of his own place, the Pacific Northwest, where he's lived since his early 20's. "There is something poignant about this area," he admitted. But as always his sympathies were hedged, his intelligences unsettling.

"It's poignant," he went on, "because it recalls for people our age the kind of countryside we remember from around maybe 1963. I mean, the way life seems basically manageable out here — that's what we'd like to think it was like all the time back in our own childhood."

And locals pay a price, he point out, for the way they've extended the environment of their childhoods. "The Northwest is comfortable largely because it's not that successful. I mean, Portland does have a posh, civilized quality that's honestly unique, but it's only got that because it hasn't yet been developed. To call it a 'livable city' is also to say that, economically, it's just scraping by."

Gibson made the comparison to Los Angeles in the early 1960s, when he'd visited briefly. "In those days, L.A. was the livable city. The countryside was gorgeous, the freeways worked. Anybody who thinks the future in my books is hard to take, well, they should just take a look at what's happened in L.A."

The point was, all contemporary cities suffer the same pressures — yet Gibson acknowledges that his imagination's fueled by the idiosyncrasies of specific locales. "On the face of it, my work would seem to argue against regionalism, and yet people in all the books have regional identities. The characters from L.A., for instance, they think of themselves as from L.A."

He saw this element as another reflection of global trends. "As the world spins an ever-denser umbrella of instantaneous communications," Gibson pointed out, "beneath that umbrella there's an increased splitting into ever-smaller groups." He mentioned the breakaway republics of the Soviet Union and Yugoslavia. "In my books, even when a character's way out in the grid, they're still from New Jersey or Finland or someplace. They're still saying things like 'Be there in a New York minute.'"

When it came to identifying his own root place, Gibson once again upset expectations. "I kinda suspect," he said, "that if I ever decide I'm a regional writer, I'll decide that I'm southern." Southern? Like Faulkner, like Flannery O'Connor? But Gibson was raised mostly in Virginia, and certainly his fiction has a Dixie fondness for the grotesque. It doesn't take too great a stretch to see cyberspace as Yoknapatawpha County laid out like a video game, with a soundtrack from the Velvet Underground.

The South may be intrinsic to Gibson's sensibility, but the Northwest provided the room to develop. "This is the one place I can think of," he said, "where spending day after day sitting in your room writing seems like a halfway reasonable thing to do. I mean, there's something so down and introspective about the way things look in winter."

He recalled an sf conference in Portland. "The event was down by the river, a hotel there. It was February or something, wintertime." One evening he and another writer found themselves on a balcony over the Willamette. "And you couldn't see four feet past the railing. We knew that the river was somewhere out there, Mt. Hood, all that scenery. But we couldn't see anything except fade to black.

"I mean," he laughed, "if a person can't write when he's faced with *that*, he might as well give it up."

It seems a durable perception. Writing may well be like that: an imaginative means towards shapes beyond the range of the naked eye. But once again, Gibson made it a point to shake up the insight before it started to feel oppressive.

"Actually," he went on, "I'm not sure I thought that up. I believe it was the guy with me, a good writer named Tom Maddox...."

Solution: The Permanent Present

Gibson made an honest effort, in our tatterdemalion exchanges. When we talked about the Northwest it was clear he'd done his homework, he'd been thinking. If at times the man indulged in a brief bob and weave, evasive action, in retrospect that too seems telling. For just as he claimed, this author isn't a science fiction novelist in the narrow sense. Nor is he a pastiche of Pynchon and anyone else, nor an old counterculturalist going moldy under Vancouver rains. What he is, is a *storyteller*.

Gibson's uneasiness with the definitions into which critics try to fit him is integral to the narrative craft. Stories aren't about defining exactly, but rather about re-defining, unexpectedly. In a famous, ancient instance, a tortoise is redefined as faster than a hare — and in Aesop's time, the tortoise coming in first must have seemed like the wildest science fiction imaginable. Good prose drama exists in a permanent present, in other words, grappling with what hippie theologians used to call "situational ethics." In contemporary fiction, few ethics might more fairly be termed *situational* than the compromises Gibson's people hammer out, and his refusal to be pigeonholed, throughout our conversations, was an honest author's application of the same difficult principles to himself.

A MEETING OF PARALLEL LINES

BY R.P. JONES

PARALLELISM and the long line in American poetry began in 1855 when a Brooklyn printer set, printed, and published one thousand copies of twelve poems, with preface; this first edition of *Leaves of Grass* used a wide page to allow its long lines to run to conclusion and a poetic structure, parallelism, resembling that of the Psalms. The style remained uniquely Whitman's for a century. Then, in 1957 William Everson wrote *River-Root*, a book-length poem relying on parallelism, a style characterized by parallel sentence structure and repeated grammatical patterns, the ancient and traditional style found in the poetry of the Old Testament.

Everson went to work in his father's print shop, The Everson Printery in Selma, California, as soon as he was old enough to work. He learned to set type and feed the Chandler platen press, but little else. Only later, when he became a poet and learned to appreciate the printed word, did he realize his lost opportunities.

In January 1943 after World War II broke out, Everson was "drafted" into a camp for conscientious objectors in Waldport, Oregon. The Waldport Camp had been chosen by the Selective Service as a site to intern writers and artists, "in hopes" as Kenneth Rexroth suggested "that they would mold away." In Waldport, Everson says, "I undertook my first real printing."

The camp already had a monthly publication called *The Tide*, but a radical group including Harold Hackett, Glen Coffield, and Larry Simons soon began an underground weekly sheet called *The Untied* which ran Everson's anti-war poems as inserts under the title of *The War Elegies*. Ten of these were later run separately, stapled together with covers, and issued as *Ten War Elegies,* their first publication. When another internee brought a small Kelsay press with him, the group published Coffield's *The Horned Moon* on it. Then Simons discovered an old Challenge-Gorden platen press in a second-hand store in Waldport; the group bought it for $70, moved it out to the camp, and began to print in earnest. After Joe Kalal, an experienced pressman, was transferred to Waldport from Michigan, Everson's *The Waldport Poems* were printed with linoleum blocks by Clayton James. Later, when Kalal decided not to print for them anymore, Everson was left to print and do all the presswork himself. During one of his furloughs from camp, he found a large Washington hand press in San Francisco and sold his insurance policy to get it. Everson's interests in poetry and printing had come together.

He was discharged after three years on July 23, 1946, and returned to California where he got a job as a janitor in the library at the University of California, Berkeley. He was soon shifted to the U.C. Press, still a janitor. There he had a chance to consolidate what he remembered from working in his father's shop in Selma and what he had learned printing at Waldport.

There, also, Everson had a chance to read everything available in the U.C. Library on handpress printing. In a 1965 interview with Ruth Teiser, he recalls: "From books I learned the whole art: paper making, type founding, ink making, how to operate the press. I read all the manuals in order to get the history, in order to get oriented. I devoured them like a man obsessed." At Berkeley he established The Equinox Press with the Washington hand press. He then moved on to master the art of book binding and, later, damping paper. In 1951 he completed printing *Triptych for the Living* and found his Order, the Dominicans at St. Albert's, as a lay brother, Brother Antoninus, and went on to print his best piece of work, the Psalter. He tells Teiser that he wanted to contribute "to the life of the Church both as a writer and as a craftsman." The first major translation since the Vulgate some 1500 years ago provided him with "a great moment, from the printer's point of view."

As Brother Antoninus, Everson began to print the Novum Psalterium PII XII. As a poet concerned with rhythms and phrasing, working so closely with the language of the Psalter left an impression. By the fall of 1957 when he was writing *River-Root,* he had mastered the parallel style.

As a printer involved in the aesthetics of design, of making the line fit the page, Brother Antoninus would have been engaged in quite a different way. The psalms came into being through a long oral tradition; they originated in the mouth and were meant for the ear. The printer's ultimate concern is visual — the book, set in print, on paper, for the eye.

As both poet and printer, Everson's relationship with his material was more problematic. In a talk given in 1976 for National Book Week, Everson speaks as a printer: "When you get two aesthetic maniacs on a collision course, one, the poet with his absolute vision of what his poem ought to look like, and the printer, knowing damn well for certain what his book is *going* to look like, it's crucifixion, really."

Everson must have been especially aware of the two warring points of view because in 1976, the year of these reflections, a fine edition of his *River-Root / A Syzygy for the Bicentennial of These States* was being designed by Thomas Whitridge for Oyez Press in Berkeley. As a poet writing for the ear, Everson no doubt had his own sense of how the long line should run out to its conclusion; as a printer he was of another mind: "…when printing my own poems I am not above sacrificing them to the printer's art. That's a fact. I'm not proud of it, as a poet. But as a printer I find myself doing it. After all, the printing is the final process, and has the last say."

River-Root shows us how Everson transformed what he handled as a printer into the other art of his calling as poet. The poem offers more than its story would suggest: man and woman meet, marry, consummate the marriage, have four children, come together a final, climactic time in the act of creation, then sleep and wake. "And smiling he stands up beside the bed, and pulls on his shirt." These activities are set against a backdrop of the River beginning at the headwaters of the Missouri, running down through the Mississippi, and draining finally into the Gulf. It is simple and clear; yet it attempts — and accomplishes — much.

The poem begins with the origins of water:

River Root. as even under high drifts, those wind-
        grappled cuts of the rockies,
One listening will hear, far down below, the softest seep-
        age, a new melt, a faint draining,

And know for certain that this is the tip, this though the
    leastest trace,
Is indeed the uttermost inch of the River.

Or on cloud-huddled days up there shut in white dense-
    ness,
Where peaks in that blindness call back and forth to each
    other,
Skim but a finger along a twig, slick off the moist,
A mere dampness the cloud has left, a vague wetness.
But still you know this too is a taking, this too can be sea,
The active element, pure inception, the residual root of
    the River.

Then the River below is seen from a transcontinental flight:

Flying over at dusk on a clear day, trending across it
Coiled below, a shimmer of light, sinuous, the quicksilver
    runner,
Deep-linking nerve of the vast continent, a sleeping
    snake.
You follow it down as the light fails, massive, majestic,
Thick and inert, recumbent, torpid with sentient power.
Slowly night takes it. When darkness drops on the valley
The River, iridescent, beats on through hot clay,
Its need and its passion dreaming far forward a full thou-
    sand miles:
Its head in the uterine sea.

Everson was not at the headwaters, but flying above them; and
those waters were not in his native California, but Montana. Still, his
commitment to the particulars of his own region — *and language* —
lets him render a landscape he is not rooted in with detail. Extending
the imagination "dreaming far forward" is what the poem asks of us.

The River runs on drawing us south and downstream as the images accumulate until they make it a major figure in the poem.

A closer look shows parallels to Genesis. While winging through
the firmament, Everson distinguishes "the waters that were under the
firmament, from those that were above the firmament" (Gen.1:7), by
showing the moisture on twig and fern as they become the sources of
the River and the "cloud-huddled...white dampness" of the upper
waters. Everson further shows us "the fowls of the air" and "the beasts

of the earth" going about their business of increasing and multiplying. And, of course, the man, the woman, and the dream.

Even the formal syntax of *River-Root* reminds us of the Douay Old Testament. Its tone celebrates beginnings in the new Eden, America, the vast new land of promise. Everson points us in this direction in his "Foreword" to the soft-bound edition: "Its appearance in this bicentennial year…is therefore appropriate because…the root energies of the nation seem to cry out for renewal, restoring a people's faith in their possibilities." He as much as confesses to the parallel in the limited Whitridge edition's "Afterword" where he tells us that he forsook his native West Coast "to situate the action of his poem and its protagonists, his New Adam and New Eve, on the Mississippi, Father of Waters…the region of his parents." His "American version of Paradise Regained" would portray redemption in phallic terms.

By encouraging us to consider the parallels with Genesis, the poem supplies a religious and historical background focusing our attentions on the meaning of the physical acts rather than the acts themselves.

Since *River-Root* is a love poem concerned with procreation as much as Genesis is concerned with creation, we might expect to find similar parallels to the Canticle. Both Solomon's Canticle and Everson's poem concern themselves with the union between man and woman, bride and bridegroom, but several specific parallels seem worth mentioning. The Canticle presents the bride as "black but beautiful" (Cant. 1:4) and says "Do not consider me that I am brown" (Cant. 1:5), while the beloved is described as "white and ruddy, chosen out of thousands" (Cant. 5:10); in *River-Root* "the man/Sleeps by the woman, husband by wife, blond by dark…."

River-Root and the Canticle both show scenes of discontent. First the Canticle (5:2-6):

> I sleep and my heart watcheth: the voice of my beloved
> knocking: Open to me, my sister, my love, my
> dove, my undefiled: for my head is full of dew, and
> my locks of the drops of the night.
> I have put off my garment, how shall I put it on? I have
> washed my feet, how shall I defile them?
> My beloved put his hand through the *key* hole, and my
> bowels were moved at his touch.
> I arose to open to my beloved: my hands dropped with

myrrh, and my fingers were full of the choicest myrrh.

I opened the bolt of my door to my beloved; but he had turned aside, and was gone. My soul melted when he spoke: I sought him, and found him not: I called him and he did not answer me.

Then *River-Root*:

And she wakens.
For there is a touch, a nudge and provocation, a slow alerting,
And in that alertness a growing tenseness.
It runs through the marrow, and out of that nerving, in ponderous sleep,
They roll together.

Stark, the innominate phallos
Knocks at the door.

And the phallos, knocking,
Finds a slow invitational yielding entrance,
A let of approval, and is roused: his body's stem,
The root of their love, stemmed out of the male, gropes through the dark,
The labial embracement.

And now they waken.

It has been between them a night this night of discontent, starving, and many a day.

Since both Solomon and Everson draw their images largely from nature, we should expect some likeness; again the Canticle (2:11, 13-14):

For winter is now past, the rain is over and gone.

...

The fig tree hath put forth her green figs: the vines in flower yield their sweet smell. Arise, my love, my beautiful one, and come:
My dove in the clefts of the rock, in the hollow places of the wall, shew me thy face, let thy voice sound in my ears....

Then *River-Root:*

> Out in the orchard, in the deep of earth,
> Inch by inch the root going down gropes towards discov-
>   ery,
> Its delicate nerve probing crevices of stone, the denseness
>   of granite,
> Seeking its own way through.

The seasonal similarities might be accidental, but "clefts of the rock" and "crevices of stone" seem too close to be. The similarities continue through listings of anatomical parts, even to posture.

If the comparable images are suggestive, even more so are the similarities of form. Robert Lowth first described the poetic form of the Old Testament poetry as *parallelismus membrorum* (parallelism of members) in *De Sacra Poesi Hebraeorum*, 1753. Verses and sentences line up in parallels that compliment or repeat, contradict or contrast, express cause and effect, or extend and build — sometimes through several verses — to climax. One hundred and thirty years later in *Isaiah of Jerusalem*, Matthew Arnold noted that Hebrew poetry "is a poetry, as is well known, of parallelism; it depends not on meter and rhyme but on a balance of thought, conveyed by a corresponding balance of sentence; and the effect of this can be transferred to another language." And more recently, Ralph Gehrke's translation of Claus Westermann's *The Psalms: Structure, Content and Message*, emphasizes the primacy of thought in the ancient poetry where the Hebrews rhymed sentences rather than words or syllables so that rhyme involved a recurrence of meaning rather than sound. If we think of the sentence instead of the word as the primary unit of thought and speech, "thought-rhymes (or sentence-rhymes) called parallelism" can more easily be understood as a sophisticated form of metaphor, a comparison of complete actions or perceptions.

The Psalms rely on vivid sensory images of natural events to convey a personal understanding of the extra-ordinary and unnameable. Their God was no abstraction; he was their shepherd who made them lie down in green pastures and led them beside the still waters; he prepared a table before them in the presence of their enemies and made their cups run over. The Twenty-third Psalm asserts the qualities of Yahweh, simply and plainly. Parallel thought express the supernatural in terms of the natural, and seek, through what was known, the unknowable mysteries.

Everson's parallelism, like his imagery, is Biblical. He tells us in the Whitridge "Afterword" that "the basic situation within which the poem is conceived…he caught a glimpse of supernal reality, the American version of Paradise Regained."

We read Genesis, or the Canticle, or the Psalms and are moved to see the world through ancient eyes as the poems recreate the original events with their emotional and, perhaps, religious content. We feel the continuity of human experience when the images and patterns of association and insight become ours as we read and our imaginations dream far backward.

This is why the classics are retranslated by each generation. But here they are re-vised, seen again, and in a new land. As Everson looks about him for the face of God, he sees "those wind-grappled cuts of the Rockies," and "when darkness drops on the valley…:"

> For in his call-up of resources he gathers behind him all
>   he holds:
> The nodes of his life, the myriad factors that fashioned
>   his fate,
> And all nature…

And at the climax of the poem:

> And the finger of God
> Inscribes on the uterine wall of the night
> Its prophesy of life
>
> And they fall.
> The great cities of their mutual awareness are
>   earthquaked under.
> All over their sky the apocalyptic constellations
> Shatter and fall down, splashing a million meanings
> In the depths of their night.
>
>   …

> Enraptured on floodtide,
> The man and the woman, two continents athwart,
> Return to the shoals of their contemplation.
> In the drenched flesh, in the fabric beyond the flesh,
> They have touched transcendence, a syzygy

Greater than wonder ever could know.
There is nothing other.

River-Root performs a syzygy in many ways. It couples ancient and contemporary prosody, Biblical and American imagery; it addresses the enduring mysteries of love, creation, belief.

Everson's transcendental relationship with the land, the life-giving waters, and his prophetic vision distinguish his way of looking as Western, derived from his roots in California. But his own "need and its passion dreaming far forward" encompasses the headwaters of the River in Montana, and his reintroduction to printing, which eventually led him back to the Psalter and the parallel style of Hebrew poetry, began at Waldport. *River-Root* re-presents our mythic origins by reaching back to our initial explanation of creation in Genesis, and to one of our earliest love poems, the Canticle. The form stretches back through the original American poem, *Leaves of Grass*, to those same Hebrew patterns of expression that gave Whitman his poetic form. Here in the West vast landscapes define us. And Everson has given voice to that archetypal Western need to participate with God and the expanse of creation. Waldport led Everson to combine the often opposed obsessions of poet and printer, preparing him — like Whitman before him — to dream beyond the limits of each. Only art can transcend the laws of the universe so the whole can be greater than the sum of its parts, and parallel lines meet.

SORRY, WE DON'T TAKE WESTERNS

BY MARY CLEARMAN BLEW

IN 1972 I SENT one of my first short stories to a prestigious national magazine and got it back almost by return mail. Written across the printed rejection form was this note: *Sorry, we don't take Westerns.*

The title of that story was "I beat the Midget," and a part of it had been born during the summer I was seventeen and my father had decided I should break a Shetland stallion to ride. For me the experience had been equal parts humiliation — my feet dragged the ground when I rode the Midget, what if somebody from school *saw* me? — and fear; the Midget might be pint-sized, but he was cold-mouthed and powerful, and when he bowed his neck and stampeded, I couldn't stop him. Out of those wild sidehill rides on the Midget, as he crashed through timber, thornbrush, and windfall with the bit in his teeth, with blue sky revolving and pine stubs breaking over my head, came the feelings I drew upon years later to tell the story of a boy's anger at his father, his frustration with an animal that could return none of his feelings, and his recognition of his own capacity to inflict pain.

I don't think that kind of rejection note would be written today. In the space of twenty years, our idea of the West, and of writing about the West, has changed radically. It is not just that gunslingers have gone out of style or that we have become too cynical to believe in the clear-cut virtues of *High Noon.* Nor — contrary to the outraged letters that pepper the journals of Western history — are the new writers of the West necessarily its destroyers. The growing awareness among historians and writers that the story of the West is not told in epic alone, nor in one voice, nor contained in any mythos, has exploded the old formulae and cleared space for the stories the men and women who lived through the process called "the frontier" knew all along.

It has been pointed out many times before now that one of the most profound developments in recent Western literature has been the emergence of talented Native American writers who have taught us to listen to a story that runs counter to the old myth of frontier settlement. But a remarkable achievement of contemporary novelists like James Welch and Louise Erdrich is their reinvention of a fictional past in which the voices of an older generation of writers — D'arcy McNickle, for example, or Mourning Dove — have a context. And in this context, a wealth of Indian oral literature emerges as the heritage of the many and varied people who hadn't been sitting around yawning while they waited for Lewis and Clark to show up and assign them a part in the Westward Movement.

Telling a story is a way we have of giving shape to ourselves out of chaos. The storyteller selects, discards, arranges, and rearranges the myriad details that clamor for telling. A new arrangement, a new story, another version of the way things are. Contemporary writers of fiction owe a lot to the oral historians and social historians who have helped to retrieve the memories and the written records of ordinary men and women and locate them in a past that seems incomparably richer and more diverse than it did twenty years ago. The voices of women in particular now resound far beyond the old stereotypes, generating a wide range of novels, stories, and memoirs dealing with women's experience in the West; a few of my recent personal favorites include Shannon Applegate (*Skookum*), Molly Gloss (*The Jump-Off Creek*), Pauline Mortensen (*Back Before the World Turned Nasty*).

Writers in the West are reconsidering the old assumptions about property and stewardship, individualism and self-reliance. Our contemporary stories are about families and cultural inheritance during a hundred hard years of farming and ranching, or about disconnections and disturbing visions in the urban West, or about the diminishing natural world and our place in it. These stories are remarkable not because they are new, but because there are so many of them and because they can be told simultaneously. Contemporary fiction about the West is complex, diverse, rich, and various in ways that barely seemed possible twenty years ago.

Nothing in the way we live now is as simple as it once seemed. But as our context expands, so does our sense of ourselves. If we are to have a future, that future may depend on our understanding of past and place. For me, the recent wealth of books written about the place where I live is a source of hope for a future.

CREDITS

Greg Bear is an author of science fiction and fantasy, married to Astrid Anderson Bear and the father of two, Erik and Alexandra. He has published sixteen books and has been awarded a Nebula, a Hugo, and the Prix Apollo. His books include *Queen of Angels, Infinity Concerto, Beyond Heaven's River, Blood Music, Tangents,* and *Eternity.*

Mary Clearman Blew, born in Lewistown, Montana, teaches creative writing at Lewis-Clark State College in Lewiston, Idaho. Her books are *Lambing Out and Other Stories, Runaway,* and a series of essays, *All But the Waltz.*

Omar Castañeda teaches at Western Washington University and is the author of *Cunuman,* an adult novel, and *Among the Volcanoes* for young adults. His forthcoming books include a sequel to the latter and a children's picture book *Esperanza's Weave* published by Lee & Low.

John Domini is the author of *Bedlam,* a book of short stories. He teaches creative writing at Linfield College in McMinnville, Oregon, and has written criticism for local and national publications, including *The New York Times, New Republic,* and *Willamette Week.*

Sharon Doubiago lives in Ashland, Oregon. Her books of poetry include *Hard Country, South America Mi Hija, Oedipus Drowned,* and *Psyche Drives the Coast, Poems 1975-1987. The Book of Seeing With One's Own Eyes* is a book of stories.

William Everson's books include *River-Root, Archetype West, Earth Poetry, The Engendering Flood, The Mate-Flight of Eagles, The Excesses of God: Robinson Jeffers As a Religious Figure, Man-Fate: The Swan Song of Brother Antoninus,* and *The Masks of Drought.*

William Gibson has authored, among others, *Neuromancer, Mona Lisa Overdrive, Burning Chrome, Count Zero,* and *The Miracle Worker.* He co-authored *The Difference Engine* with Bruce Sterling.

Terri Lee Grell lives in Toutle, Washington, and is the editor and publisher of *Lynx,* a quarterly journal of renga. Her work has been published in *Mirrors, Exquisite Corpse, Next Exit, Lost and Found Times, The Bellingham Review* and the anthology *Narrow Road to Renga.* She will be doing an interview with Tess Gallagher and a Romanian woman for the next *Left Bank.*

A.B. Guthrie is the author of *The Big Sky, The Way West, These Thousand Hills, Fair Land, Fair Land, Four Miles from Ear Mountain* and *Murder in the Cotswolds.*

Lowell Jaeger lives in Bigfork, Montana. He has a new chapbook, *Law of the Fish,* and two collections of poems in print: *War on War* and *Hope Against Hope,* both from Utah State University Press. Lowell teaches at Flathead Valley Community College in Kalispell, Montana, and his awards include the 1991 Montana Council of the Arts Fellowship for poetry and a 1986 grant from the National Endowment for the Arts.

R.P. Jones, born in New York City, teaches poetry and literature at Pacific Lutheran University in Tacoma, Washington. His books of poetry are *Waiting For Spring* (Circinatum Press, 1978) and *The Rest Is Silence* (Broken Moon Press, 1984). He has given writing workshops at McNeil Island Federal Penitentiary and the Purdy Corrections Center for Women.

John Keeble's essay is excerpted from *Out of the Channel: The Exxon Valdez Oil Spill in Prince William Sound.* His four novels are *Crab Canon* (Grossman, 1971), *Mine* (with Ransom Jeffery, Grossman, 1974), *Broken Ground* (Harper and Row, 1980) and *Yellowfish* (Harper and Row, 1987). He scripted *To Write and Keep Kind,* a public television documentary (KCTS Seattle) on the life and work of Raymond Carver.

William Kittredge's stories have appeared in *Atlantic Monthly, The Iowa Review, Northwest Review, The Syracuse Scholar,* and *Triquarterly.* His books include *We Are Not in This Together,* and *Owning It All,* and with Annick Smith, he edited *The Last Best Place: A Montana Anthology.* His new book will be published spring 1992.

Craig Lesley was born in The Dalles, Oregon, and teaches at Clackamas Community College. He is the author of *Winterkill* and *Riversong*, and is the editor of *Talking Leaves*. He is now working on a novel of small-town life in the West. In 1984 he received the American Golden Spur Award from the Western Writers Association for *Winterkill*, and received an honorary Doctor of Letters from Whitman College.

Roy Miki and **Cassandra Kobayashi** played an active role in the Japanese Canadian redress movement as community representatives and as members of the NAJC Strategy Committee that negotiated the Redress Settlement. They are both sansei (third-generation Japanese Canadians). **Roy Miki** teaches in the English Department at Simon Fraser University where he edits *West Coast Line*. **Cassandra Kobayashi** is a Vancouver lawyer. She has collaborated with Roy Miki on many projects on Japanese Canadians, including *Spirit of Redress: Japanese Canadians in Conference*.

Jacqueline Moreau: "I became acquainted with members of the river people in 1985 while on assignment for United Press International. Shortly thereafter I decided to photograph these Columbia River Indians in greater depth. The result was a traveling exhibit, 'The River People,' made possible with a grant in 1987 from the Metropolitan Arts Commission in Portland. Over a ten year period I freelanced as a photographer for numerous newspapers. I now work seasonally as a forest fire lookout in the Cascade Mountain Range and live in the Columbia River Gorge in Washington."

Nancy Lord is the author of *Survival* (from Coffee House Press), and *The Compass Inside Ourselves: Short Stories*. She fishes commercially in Alaska and traveled to the Soviet Far East in 1989. "Magadan Luck" was previously printed in *Uncommon Waters: Women Write About Fishing* (Seal Press).

Norman Maclean's first books of stories — *A River Runs Through It and Other Stories* — was published when he was 73 years-old. In the fall of 1992, The University of Chicago will bring out his book *Young Men & Fire*, a non-fiction novel account of the Mann Gulch fire.

Richard Manning covered environmental news for the *Missoulian* newspaper. After he wrote a series investigating the timber industry, the newspaper gave in to pressure from those companies and removed Manning from his beat. The *Missoulian* won the C.B. Blethen Award for investigative journalism (Manning's third) for the series. The essay here is an excerpt from his book *Last Stand: Logging, Journalism, and the Case for Humility.*

Doug Marx is a poet, freelance journalist, teacher, professional land surveyor, and family man. His poems have appeared in such publications as *COLUMBIA—a Magazine of Poetry & Prose, Hubbub, Mississippi Mud,* and *Alaska Quarterly Review.* He's a frequent contributor to the *Oregonian, Willamette Week,* and *Writer's NW.*

Penelope Reedy is the editor and publisher of *The Redneck Review of Literature* published since 1975 from Twin Falls, Idaho. Temporarily published from Milwaukee, Wisconsin, the magazine's focus is contemporary western American literature.

Paul Richards is a former member of the Montana House of Representatives, and a newsman with The Associated Press and a stringer for United Press International. He currently writes and lives in the Elkhorn Mountains near Boulder, Montana.

William Stafford was Oregon's Poet Laureate for many years. His numerous books of poetry include *Traveling Through the Dark, An Oregon Message,* and *The Long Sigh the Wind Makes.*

Wallace Stegner has published over twenty works of fiction and nonfiction. His novel, *Angle of Repose,* won the Pulitzer Prize, and another novel, *Spectator Bird,* the National Book Award. *The American West as Living Space* and *Crossing to Safety* were both published in 1987. Other books include *Joe Hill, Mormon Country, Recapitulation, Second Growth, The Sound of Mountain Water, Wolf Willow,* and *The Women on the Wall.*

Robert Stubblefield attended Clackamas Community College and Eastern Oregon State College. He was a two-time winner (1989 and 1990) of Clackamas Community College Writer's Fiction Contest. Robert has published two short stories in *Rhapsody* and was the assistant editor of *Oregon East.*

Paul Zarzyski is a poet and rodeo cowboy hailing from Montana. He has published his work in over thirty journals, magazines, and anthologies. Among his four collections are *The Make-Up of Ice* and *Roughstock Sonnets.*

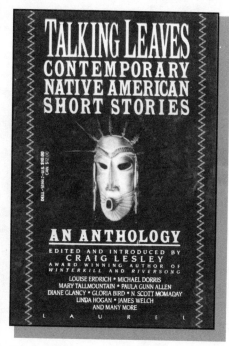

POET™
MAGAZINE

is looking for
poets and writers
just like you.

For free guidelines and contest information,
send your request with a self-addressed,
stamped envelope to

Cooper House Publishing Inc.
P.O. Box 54947, Dept. LB
Oklahoma City, OK 73154

A Cooper House publication

Clark City Press

LAW OF THE RANGE
PORTRAITS OF OLD-TIME BRAND INSPECTORS
by Stephen Collector
with an introduction by Annick Smith
Cloth, $45.00

DEATH AND THE GOOD LIFE
A Mystery by Richard Hugo
with an introduction by James Welch
Paper, $9.95

THE MUDDY FORK & OTHER THINGS
Short Fiction and Nonfiction by James Crumley
Paper, $12.95

JUST BEFORE DARK
Collected Nonfiction by Jim Harrison
Cloth, $24.95

THE ANGLER'S COAST
Stories by Russell Chatham
with a prologue by Thomas McGuane
Cloth, $34.95

DARK WATERS
Essays, Stories and Articles
by Russell Chatham
Illustrated, Paper, $14.95

 Clark City Press

POST OFFICE BOX 1358 LIVINGSTON, MONTANA 59047
(800) 835-0814 FAX (406) 222-3371

Distributed to the trade by Consortium (800) 283-3572

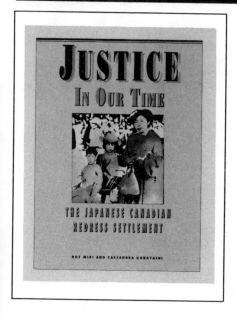